"The bays a

"Dad always wanted to learn to sail. When he retired he bought a yacht and ten acres near the water."

Her eyes lit up. "I love sailing, although I haven't been out on the harbor in ages."

He gazed into her striking eyes, the same color as her stunning blue dress. No wonder she was the first person he'd noticed when he arrived at the party.

"I'd like to be out on the water every weekend," he said, "and I've just brought my yacht back from Port Stephens."

"You have a yacht." She shuffled closer to him as the crowd pressed in behind her.

"She's a little beauty and sails like the wind." He leaned forward so she could hear him above the party chatter. "I'm taking her out on the harbor next weekend. Come with me."

"Why?" Surprise filled her voice.

"Why not? You love sailing and my yacht needs a run on the harbor." He held her gaze, giving her a big smile. "It'll be fun."

Books by Narelle Atkins

Love Inspired Heartsong Presents

Falling for the Farmer
The Nurse's Perfect Match
The Doctor's Return
Her Tycoon Hero

NARELLE ATKINS

lives in Canberra, Australia, with her husband and children. Her love of romance novels was inspired by her grandmother's extensive collection. After discovering inspirational romances, she decided to write stories of faith and romance. A regular at her local gym, she also enjoys traveling and spending time with family and friends.

NARELLE ATKINS

Her Tycoon Hero

Recycling programs for this product may not exist in your area.

ISBN-13: 978-0-373-48734-9

Her Tycoon Hero

This edition published by arrangement with Love Inspired Books.

www.Harlequin.com

Printed in U.S.A.

Bear with each other and forgive one another
if any of you has a grievance against someone.
Forgive as the Lord forgave you.

—*Colossians* 3:13

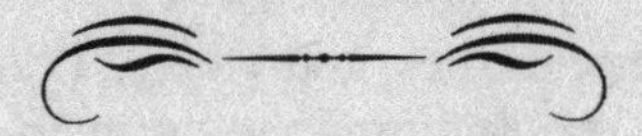

For my husband, Jay, who has believed in this story
for a long time and is my biggest supporter.
You're my hero and an inspiration to me. I love you.

Acknowledgments

I appreciate the help and support I've received
from many people during the writing of this book.
Mary Hawkins, my lovely mentor and dear friend
who provided invaluable feedback on this story.
Susan Diane Johnson and Stacy Monson,
my wonderful critique partners. Many thanks to
Laura O'Connell for her insightful critiques. I also
thank the many contest judges who generously
gave their time to provide helpful feedback and
encouragement on earlier versions of this story.

I thank my reader friends for their helpful feedback
and support: Jen B, Lisa B, Raylee B, Karinne C,
Tracey H, Daniela M, Heather M and Merlyn S.
Thanks also to my father-in-law, Kerry, for providing
research opportunities and advice on the
sailing scenes. Any errors are mine.

A special thank-you to my editor, Kathy Davis,
and the team at Harlequin.

Chapter 1

Everything was in place for her sister's engagement party.

Cassie Beaumont pulled out a stool from under the granite counter in a quiet corner of her father's enormous kitchen, resting her weary body on the cushioned seat. Platters of gourmet appetizers filled the kitchen and the large round table in the breakfast nook. She'd given the caterers detailed instructions and they were ahead of schedule, preparing additional food at the island in the center of the kitchen. Everything was going brilliantly. Dad and Laura should be happy.

She twisted a lock of blond hair around her finger and glanced at the time illuminated on the microwave oven. Eight-fifteen. Guests had started arriving at eight.

The aroma of mini quiches fresh from the oven stirred her appetite. She'd only eaten a muesli bar for lunch, squeezed in between appointments. Her feet ached from rushing around at the hotel. Fridays were always hectic and today had been no exception. Snatching a few minutes to rest her feet felt like a precious gift.

Her father strode through the busy kitchen, coming to a halt a few feet in front of her. "Cassandra, I've been looking for you everywhere."

She clenched her fists and tipped up her chin, pasting a smile on her face. What had she done wrong this time? "What's up?"

John frowned, shoving his hands in the pockets of his

conservative gray suit and lowering his voice. "Laura and Greg are expecting a big turnout. Do you have enough staff?"

"It's all organized." She'd made sure he would have no reason to worry. She'd scrutinized all the arrangements, leaving nothing to chance.

His gaze swept over his spacious kitchen. "Have you ordered enough food?"

She pointed to the trays of canapés lined up on the nearby table, keeping her tone even. "There's a mountain of food ready to be served. I have it all under control." Thankfully her competent catering staff couldn't overhear their conversation.

"I expect this party to be perfect." An icy tone permeated his low voice.

"It will be." She held his gaze, refusing to be intimidated. She'd worked hard to pull this party together. Why couldn't he acknowledge her efforts with a thank-you?

He leaned back against the counter and crossed his arms. "I told Laura she should have hired a professional party planner."

"And what am I?" Pain flooded her heart and old insecurities resurfaced. Her professional role as an events manager for a five-star Sydney hotel wasn't good enough for him. What would it take to convince him she'd changed? She was twenty-six years old and no longer the unreliable daughter with a drinking problem.

"I offered to pay top dollar for the right person." He smoothed back the few remaining strands of gray hair on his balding head. "Instead I find you in the kitchen worrying about food."

"Dad, I'm Laura's maid of honor. She asked me to organize her party and it will be a big success."

He snorted. "We'll see. At least you're not drinking on the job."

Her jaw fell slack, his stinging words further damaging

their fragile relationship. Did he want to push her away and out of his life forever?

She sucked in a deep breath, determined to prove him wrong. "I haven't had a drink in nearly two years and my faith helps me to stay on track. Why can't you believe me when I tell you I'm a different person now?"

"That's what your grandmother used to say."

She stood, placing her hands on her hips. "I'm not like Grandma."

"She went to church every week and it never did *her* any good."

"I'm dealing with my problems." Her grandmother had struggled for many years with alcoholism and liver disease.

"You don't need religion. You just need someone to keep you in line."

Like a husband. His unspoken words cut open another raw wound. She straightened her spine, standing taller. "I'm doing okay on my own."

"Why can't you settle down like your sister?" His voice softened. "Is that too much to ask?"

She looked away, realizing she'd failed him again by her inability to find an appropriate man who met with his approval.

He uncrossed his arms and moved closer. "Why don't you stop hiding in the kitchen and mingle with Greg and Laura's friends? There must be a few good prospects here tonight."

She stepped back, frowning. Did he mean Ryan Mitchell, his right-hand man at JB Management? Had Laura been talking to Dad behind her back? "I'm capable of finding my own dates and I don't need help from you or anyone else."

He looked down his nose and let out an exasperated sigh. "I hear you loud and clear. I really hope this religious conversion of yours fixes your problems, but you'd better not screw up tonight." He threw his hands in the air and stormed out of the kitchen.

Her father's anger tore at her heart. Cassie took a deep breath and counted to ten. *Please Lord, give me patience.*

She placed her trembling palms flat on the kitchen counter and blinked away her impending tears. Her family didn't share her faith, and her difficult relationship with her father had deteriorated after she made the life-changing decision to become a Christian eighteen months ago.

She sucked in a steadying breath. Dad wanted to provide the best possible engagement party for Laura, his perfect daughter. She didn't begrudge her sister's close relationship with their father, but how could she improve her own relationship with him when they couldn't manage to hold a civil conversation for five minutes? Her head hurt from hammering it against the unbreakable wall between them.

She'd had enough. Tomorrow she would update her résumé and apply for a position in North Queensland. The job—an executive events manager at an exclusive island resort—appealed to her for many reasons. Sunshine, sandy beaches and days spent diving around the reefs. What more could she want?

Cassie stared at her younger sister's engagement cake. Would she ever meet the right man? She prayed for a husband who shared her faith and prioritized family over work. A man of honor and integrity, the exact opposite of Sean.

She shuddered, thankful she'd escaped Sean's maze of lies.

Additional waiters arrived. Satisfied with progress on the catering front, she exited the kitchen to check out the party.

Her high heels tapped on the tiled floor as she strode into the spacious living room of her father's waterfront mansion. A large number of the one hundred invited guests mingled indoors while a few others braved the cooler evening temperatures on the balcony.

Cassie gazed through a panoramic window, admiring the multimillion-dollar views of the city skyline and Sydney Harbour Bridge. Fairy lights strung around the gazebo next to the pool lit up the immaculate gardens in a soft glow.

Regret tainted her pleasure. She rarely visited her father's home and she'd already broken her promise to Laura by arguing with Dad. Would she ever learn to control her tongue?

The soothing tones of the hired jazz quartet lifted her spirits. If she avoided her father for the rest of the evening, everything should be okay.

Her sister had enough to worry about tonight. Top of her list would be wondering if their divorced parents could peacefully coexist at the party.

She scanned the room and did a double take when she spotted her parents standing together. Her father made a comment and her mother laughed with him.

Wow. But could it last?

Cassie strolled through the open French doors and onto the balcony, looking for Laura. The breeze off the harbor cooled her bare arms and her new sapphire-blue evening gown swirled around her calves.

She stumbled on the pavers as she negotiated her way down the steps to the landscaped gardens. At least her ankle didn't collapse. A few years ago she'd worn flimsy high-heeled sandals on a regular basis, often with disastrous consequences. She needed to take more care, although her sobriety made a big difference.

Her sister stood in the gazebo, her sleek dark brown hair flowing loose around her shoulders. Surrounded by friends, she held her left hand in the air and showed off her large diamond solitaire engagement ring. The joy on Laura's face spoke volumes about her love for her future husband.

A twinge of envy filled Cassie. She stamped out her uncharitable thoughts when Laura waved and raced over to her.

"Has Ryan arrived yet?" Laura asked. "I'm dying to introduce you to him."

Cassie rolled her eyes. "How would I know?"

"Maybe he's inside." Laura tilted her head sideways. "Greg said he was snowed under with work."

"I'm sure Ryan will turn up soon." He sounded like a younger version of Dad, boring and obsessed with work. Not her type.

"He'd better, considering he's going to be the best man at our wedding."

"Stop fretting. You're supposed to be enjoying a fun night."

"Okay, but I know you'll like Ryan." Laura's blue eyes sparkled. "He's gorgeous and a very good catch."

Cassie shrugged. Laura's romantic notion of the maid of honor and best man falling in love was not going to happen.

"You two are perfect for each other," Laura continued. "He recently moved back to Sydney after a three-year stint in London. Did I tell you he once dated an Aussie model?"

Cassie lifted a brow. A few years ago she might have been impressed, but now she couldn't care less. "Have you forgotten he's Sean's older brother?"

"Sean's long gone, and it's not like you dated him or anything." Laura waved away Cassie's concerns. "You're Ryan's type and you should go for it."

"What? How do you know his type?"

"Greg may have mentioned that Ryan's partial to blue-eyed blondes. Trust me—he's a class above the last few guys you've dated."

Cassie squirmed. "Life isn't all about money. I'm looking for someone who shares my faith."

"Maybe he believes in God, but who cares?" Laura flicked her brunette locks back over her shoulder. "I don't get why you're so hung up on religion."

She bit back a sharp retort. *Let it go.* Now wasn't the time to have this conversation. "Mom and Dad appear to be getting on okay." She relayed the scene she'd witnessed a few minutes earlier.

"You're kidding!" A huge smile broke out on her sister's face. "It's about time they buried the hatchet."

Cassie nodded. "Look, Greg's waving at you to join him by the pool. We can talk later." She hugged Laura before heading indoors.

Cassie meandered through the throng of guests gathered in the living room, greeting several aunts, uncles and cousins as she made her way back to the kitchen. Her parents congregated with their respective relations on opposite sides of the room. One pleasant conversation was progress and had exceeded her expectations.

A quick perusal of the kitchen reassured her that everything was fine. Happy with the caterers, she selected an iced tea from a passing waiter and returned to the living room.

A man appeared at the entrance of the room. He stood tall, with dark brown hair cropped short against his collar but styled longer at the front, sweeping back off his broad forehead. She was too far away to discern the color of his eyes but close enough to feel his commanding presence. Other heads turned his way, but he seemed oblivious to all the speculative glances.

Her gaze collided with his and a jolt of pure awareness shot through her. Something about him seemed familiar.

The crowd shifted, breaking their connection. She searched the doorway, unable to see him.

What had she been thinking, letting a handsome stranger set her pulse racing? She took a sip from her glass, her first impression of him lingering in her mind like the tangy lemon flavor of her iced tea.

Then it hit her. Could he be Ryan? The general shape of his head and jawline showed an uncanny resemblance to Sean.

She selected a mini quiche from a passing waiter and her future brother-in-law joined her.

"Thanks for organizing our party," Greg said. "You've done a fantastic job."

"My pleasure." She popped the warm pastry in her mouth.

"Your Dad's house is amazing and it's great he let us hold the party here."

She nodded, savoring the superb flavor of the quiche. "He's happy to entertain as long as someone else does the catering."

Greg grinned, glancing over her shoulder. "Here comes Laura with Ryan."

Cassie spun around and gasped. A shiver of anticipation hurtled up her spine as her gaze once again locked with his. His light gray eyes complemented his tanned complexion.

She dragged her gaze away and tried to focus her attention on her sister. A mischievous glint flickered in Laura's eyes as she made the introductions.

"Hi." Cassie shook the hand Ryan offered, his grasp warm and firm.

Ryan smiled. "Good to see you again."

It took a few moments for his words to sink in. She drew her brows together. "We've met before?"

"Please excuse us." Laura grabbed hold of Greg's arm. "It's nearly time for the speeches and cake so we'll leave you two to chat."

Ryan watched Greg and Laura disappear into the crowd. "We met a few years ago at a party." He looked her straight in the eye. "Sean introduced us and, if I remember correctly, you gave me an enthusiastic hug."

She lowered her lashes, shame cloaking her. Her partying days were a blur she'd rather forget.

"You were wearing a little black dress." A smile twitched at the corner of his mouth. "My brother kept you close by his side all night."

She cringed. Could things get any more embarrassing? She'd thrown the figure-hugging dress in the trash long ago. "Sean and I went to lots of parties." She frowned. "I'm sorry, but I don't remember."

"No worries." He stepped closer, lowering his deep voice to a whisper. "You're more beautiful than I remember."

"Thanks." Her cheeks heated and she switched her attention to his silk tie. Conservative hues of blue and green. Had he chosen the tie especially for tonight or had he been wearing it all day at the office?

She inhaled a deep breath. Why did she feel such a powerful connection with Sean's brother?

"Is something wrong?" he asked.

"It's a little awkward not remembering we'd met before."

"Okay, I confess I have an unfair advantage. Your father has a photo of you and Laura on his desk."

Did Dad display her photo to keep up appearances? Or did he care about her despite his abrupt attitude?

A ray of hope lighted inside her. *Lord, please help me find a way to mend my relationship with Dad.*

Curiosity drove her to ask the one question burning in her mind. "How's Sean doing?"

A dark look shadowed his face. "I've no idea. You're the last person to see him before he left the country. Even my parents haven't heard from him in over two years."

"Really? He hasn't contacted anyone?"

Ryan nodded, his mouth set in a grim line.

She sipped the remainder of her tea, struggling to understand why she had once contemplated Sean's crazy idea of turning their friendship into a more serious relationship. Not that they'd have stood a chance. Her drinking problems combined with his irresponsible actions had destroyed any potential for a healthy relationship or future together.

The passing of time and a clear head had revealed Sean's character flaws. But they'd been close friends, inseparable before he'd left, and she'd known another side of him. She couldn't forget or dismiss from her mind the many times he'd been caring and considerate.

"Ryan, I'm sorry about how everything turned out with Sean. I'd hoped he'd sorted himself out by now."

"My brother chose his life path and he has to live with the consequences."

Her father didn't let her forget her troubled past. The consequences seemed never ending.

Ryan's eyes softened as he met her gaze. "Do you keep in touch with any of Sean's friends?"

"Not anymore." She twirled a lock of hair around her finger. "I avoid the party scene."

"Have you heard anything about Sean's whereabouts?"

She shook her head. "I'm not interested in seeing him again."

He nodded. "You've done a great job organizing this party."

"I haven't done much." She loosened her grip on her glass, thankful he'd changed the subject. "The caterers and waiters have done most of the work."

"They deserve a bonus." He removed his jacket and draped it back over his shoulder, emphasizing the broad expanse of his chest.

She drew in a few deep breaths and tried to calm her tightly coiled nerves. She felt like a schoolgirl in the throes of her first teenage crush.

Her father began speaking into the microphone, calling Laura and Greg to join him up on the musician's dais. She welcomed the distraction from the man standing close by her side.

Dad's short, humorous speech drew plenty of laughter, even from her. But her aggravation with him remained. She'd do her best to stay out of his way.

Laura and Greg thanked everyone for coming and proceeded to cut their engagement cake.

Ryan signaled a waiter, who immediately came over.

"What can I offer you?" Ryan asked.

"I'm good, thanks." She passed her empty glass to the waiter.

Ryan selected a beverage, his eyes twinkling. "Let's go outside?"

"Sure." She should stop by the kitchen. But her staff were on top of their game and distributing cake to appreciative guests. The kitchen could wait.

She walked with Ryan toward the balcony. His honesty regarding his brother demonstrated his integrity. Sean had insisted that Ryan and his parents were critical and judgmental, but who could blame his family for being concerned about him?

Ryan came to a halt, his fingers cupping her elbow for a brief moment. "John's waving at me."

Her smile froze on her lips. *Talk about bad timing.* Why did her father need to see Ryan right now?

Chapter 2

Ryan frowned. Which deal had hit a snag this time?

John Beaumont sauntered over, annoyance shadowing his tired face. "Sorry to interrupt, Ryan, but we need to talk."

Cassie stepped away from him. "Oh, I'll go check on things in the kitchen."

Ryan turned to her, his mouth curving up as he looked into her deep blue eyes. "Please stay—this shouldn't take long."

"Two minutes at the most," John said.

"Okay." She shifted her gaze to the floor, her wavy blond locks falling forward over her face.

His breath caught in his throat. Her beauty mesmerized him, but her discomfort around her own father surprised him.

"I just received a call from London," John said.

His stomach sank. This could only mean one thing. "What's wrong?"

"The parent company has changed some of the project parameters," John said. "They need the revised projections by close of business, London time."

Ryan checked his watch, frustrated by the interruption. He hadn't transferred the latest version of the confidential files to his off-site data storage account, assuming this stage of the project was finalized. But he needed to talk to Cassie first, before he left. “I’ll go back to the office tonight.”

“Thanks.” John cast a wary glance in his daughter’s direction before returning his attention to Ryan. “I know this is bad timing and I’m sorry to cut your evening short.”

Cassie continued to stare at the floor. Why wouldn’t she even look at her father? What had gone wrong between the two of them?

“Good thing I’ve taken over this project from Greg.” He hoped to thaw the frosty atmosphere between father and daughter. “Laura would go nuts if Greg had to work tonight.”

John nodded. “I’ll pass on your apologies. See you both later.” He walked away.

Cassie’s beautiful eyes narrowed. “You really have to leave now.”

“Yes, unfortunately.” As second in command at the Sydney office, he often found himself working at all hours of the day. John was a good boss—tough but fair. Both Ryan and Greg had followed John when he set up his own management consulting company four years ago.

“I hope you won’t have to work too late.”

“Me, too.” He drained his glass. “First thing tomorrow morning I’m driving to my parents’ place for the weekend.”

“I met them once, when they came to Sydney.” She nibbled her lower lip. “Are they still at Port Stephens?”

He nodded. “They remember you.” His parents had liked Cassie and had hoped she might be a positive influence on Sean.

“The bays are beautiful.”

“Dad always wanted to learn to sail. When he retired he bought a yacht and ten acres near the water.”

Her eyes lit up. “I love sailing, although I haven’t been out on the harbor in ages.”

He gazed into her striking eyes, the same color as her

stunning blue dress. No wonder she was the first person he'd noticed when he arrived at the party.

"I'd like to be out on the water every weekend," he said, "and I've just brought my yacht back from Port Stephens."

"You have a yacht." She shuffled closer to him as the crowd pressed in behind her.

"She's a little beauty and sails like the wind." He leaned forward so she could hear him above the party chatter. "I'm taking her out on the harbor next weekend. Come with me."

"Why?" Surprise filled her voice.

"Why not? You love sailing and my yacht needs a run on the harbor." He held her gaze, giving her a big smile. "It'll be fun."

"I'll have to check my work schedule. When are you heading out?"

"Probably Sunday afternoon."

She paused, her brows knitting together. "You don't think it's a little awkward for us to be hanging out because of my history with your brother?"

"My brother is history." He clenched his fist. "He needs to come home and deal with his problems. My parents are worried sick."

"I can't imagine how awful this is for your family."

"It's tough." Every time he and his mother spoke she still asked him if he'd heard from Sean.

"I hope he returns home soon."

He nodded, anger and frustration coursing through him. Ryan needed to find his brother. Sean owed him and Dad a stack of money.

He'd heard rumors his brother was in Sydney. Sooner or later he'd track him down and make him repay his debts.

"Can I let you know next week if I'm free on Sunday?"

He nodded, handing her his business card. "My cell phone is the easiest way to contact me. Or I might see you on the ferry."

She lifted a brow. "How do you know which one I catch?"

He grinned. "Laura."

She lowered her lashes. "Why doesn't this surprise me?"

"It's all good," he said, aware of her discomfort. "Anyway, I have to run. Have a great weekend."

"You, too."

Cassie disappeared into the crowd and he spotted Laura waving at him from across the room.

Laura approached him, smiling. "Thanks for coming. Dad said you're leaving now."

"Yeah, have you seen Greg?" He'd hardly spoken to Greg all evening.

"He's around somewhere."

"I'm glad I could make it." He scanned the crowded room, searching for Greg.

"Me, too," she said. "Let's do dinner soon."

"Sounds great. Tell Greg I'll be in touch."

"Sure." Laura gave him a brief hug. "See you later."

He made a final sweeping glance of the room and found Cassie looking his way. Returning her smile, he sensed she shared his disappointment over his having to leave early.

The elegant woman he'd met tonight didn't resemble the wild girl he remembered from a few years ago. Despite everything, he wanted to get to know her better and prove to her he was nothing like his brother. The magnetic connection between them had captivated his thoughts.

She'd claimed to have no clue of his brother's whereabouts and he'd believed her, entranced by her wide-eyed innocence. Would she help him find Sean?

Being seen with Cassie might have the added benefit of drawing his brother out of hiding. She was his best lead so far, and he intended to see her again very soon.

On Tuesday morning Cassie groaned as the Manly Ferry glided away from the wharf without her. If only she'd left home ten minutes earlier.

Her plans to play tennis later today with Julia and the

singles group from church were now in doubt, even if the rain held off. She could work through her lunch break but couldn't guarantee she'd finish everything in time.

The overcast gray sky and chilly breeze off the harbor inspired her to walk faster on the path along the foreshore. She buried her hands deeper in the pockets of her full-length coat.

Her father's words plagued her thoughts. If she wanted to find a suitable husband, she had to prioritize opportunities to meet possible candidates. Playing tennis with her church friends wasn't what Dad had in mind.

She adjusted a loose hairpin and rearranged the fluffy scarf around her neck. Her cell phone beeped in her purse.

Slowing her pace, she checked the screen and almost dropped her phone as she read Ryan's message. He was catching the next ferry and had offered to buy her coffee.

Cassie smiled. Something good had come from running late. She sent him a hasty reply, thanking him in advance for a latte with one sugar.

Moments later her phone beeped again, confirming the coffee arrangements.

She walked along with an added spring in her step. He wanted to see her. Last night she'd again put off calling him to confirm the arrangements for Sunday.

She'd chided herself for feeling nervous, but a sermon on marriage a few weeks ago had stuck in her mind. Was it wise to consider dating a man who didn't go to church? Right now she had no idea if he shared her faith.

She reached the promenade leading to the wharf and shortened her stride. Numerous pigeons flew around, seeking crumbs left by the hundreds of tourists who visited Manly each day. The towering Norfolk pines swayed overhead in the salty sea breeze; their fallen needles crunched under her low-heeled boots on the paved path.

She joined the flow of commuters filing through the wharf to the boarding area as the next ferry came into view. She searched the crowd, looking for Ryan among the people milling around her.

The ferry docked at the wharf and she waited for the boarding gates to open. Still unable to see him, she moved forward and made her way to the rear of the upper deck.

She sat next to a window and reached into her leather purse to retrieve her travel-sized Bible. Hopefully she'd have time to read two or three verses before Ryan arrived with coffee.

Her hand skimmed over the spiral notebook she used to write down questions for Julia. Her best friend had led her to Christ and spent many hours helping her understand the Bible.

She opened the Gospel of Matthew, found her place and started reading.

The departure bell sounded, and a sudden feeling of awareness came over her.

Ryan headed her way, cutting a dashing figure in his unbuttoned coat and business suit.

Her heart skipped a beat and she returned his smile. The sweet aroma of coffee wafted in her direction as she lifted her purse off the spare seat beside her.

"Hey." He passed over her latte.

"Thanks." She held the warm cardboard cup, invigorated by the scent of caffeine and his presence. *He must be a morning person to be so energized this early.*

"No problem." He sat next to her, stretching out his long legs and crossing them at his ankles. He glanced at her Bible. "I didn't realize I was interrupting your reading."

"I'm all done." She tucked her Bible into her purse, having finished reading the passage in Matthew where Jesus and Peter walked on water.

The waves outside lapped around the ferry, and she marveled at Peter's faith and trust in Jesus. She wanted to experience the same depth of faith. Could she be like Peter and give up everything to follow Jesus?

She sipped her latte, remembering she'd only drunk half a mug of instant coffee earlier this morning. "This is good coffee."

He nodded. "Do you read the Bible every day?"

"I try to read during breakfast. But on days like today when I'm running late, it doesn't work out that way."

"I'd also planned to leave much earlier."

"Is my dad being a hard taskmaster?"

He laughed. "Always, but he's a good man. His dedication is the reason his company is successful."

"But his success has come at a price."

"The financial rewards are worth it."

She lifted a brow. "Maybe. Dad lives at the office and hasn't got time for a personal life." She resented the fact her father prioritized work over family. How could Ryan perceive Dad's unbalanced lifestyle as good?

Ryan's smile faded. "He has a girlfriend."

"You mean the blonde."

"I met her once and she seemed nice."

"She's nice because she sees dollar signs." Cassie sipped her latte, avoiding his penetrating gaze. "She won't last."

"How do you know?" He sat up straighter in his seat. "Have you even met her?"

She narrowed her eyes. "I know my father. If she's an important part of his life, he'd tell me. I don't even know her name."

His frown deepened. "Her name's Debbie."

Cassie shrugged. "Whatever."

"Maybe you'd know her name if you spent more time with your father." Irritation pervaded his tone.

Ouch. "It's not that simple. Anyway, if he didn't work all the time, he'd have more time to see me."

"Laura sees him a lot."

She pressed her lips together. He didn't get it. Laura had the brilliant relationship with Dad that she wanted but couldn't achieve. "My relationship with Dad is complicated," she said, uncomfortable with the way he defended her father. "Can we talk about something else?"

"Sure." He sipped his coffee. "I think it's going to be a rough ride today."

She nodded and stared out the window. Rain pelted down on the glass, obliterating the view of the headlands. Had Ryan adopted her father's obsessive work ethic? Did that explain his single status?

The rhythmic rocking of the ferry gained momentum. She unfolded her legs and placed both feet on the deck. The last thing she needed was a coffee stain on her coat.

Where did Ryan stand with God? He'd seemed comfortable with the idea of her reading the Bible, but he'd shown no interest in discussing the content.

The loudspeaker system blared to life, advising passengers to remain indoors. The ferry lurched up and then dropped. She reached for the armrest and grasped Ryan's forearm.

Startled, she withdrew her hand and gripped the edge of her seat.

"You okay?" he asked.

"I'd prefer not to wear my coffee." She gulped down the remainder of her latte.

He grinned. "This reminds me of ocean sailing, which is always more fun on windy days when the waves are huge."

"Maybe, but I prefer sailing on a calm sunny day."

"And miss out on all the fun. Why?"

"Do you really want to know?"

He raised an eyebrow. "It couldn't be that bad."

"Well, when I was eleven, Dad entered his yacht in a special event race. It was a hot day and a storm was brewing."

"All right, I concede this isn't sounding good."

She nodded. "We were on the home leg and in the lead when the yacht tacked sharply and I ended up overboard."

"Were you okay?" His face mirrored the concern in his voice.

"I could swim and Dad yelled out that he'd come back and collect me after he crossed the finish line."

"What? He left you to fend for yourself?"

"Yep. Yachts were coming at me from all directions and there was lots of lightning and thunder."

"That's really scary for an eleven-year-old."

"Dad didn't think so." She dropped her gaze to study her fingernails. "Winning the race was more important to him."

"I'm glad you survived."

"So am I." After that hair-raising experience she'd avoided sailing with Dad for a long time.

"Are we still on for Sunday? If the weather's bad, I understand if you want to bail."

"I'm not working and I don't think rain is forecast."

"Great. How about I pick you up at your place after eleven?"

She wrote her address on her business card. "What can I bring?"

"I'll fix lunch. Make sure you wear warm clothes."

"No problem." She glanced out the window, relieved to see the rain had eased off. With any luck she wouldn't get wet racing up the road to work.

"Have you eaten breakfast?"

"Sort of." If she counted the apple she'd eaten while rushing around her apartment.

"Why don't we grab a bite to eat before work? There's a little café with great views just up from the quay."

She widened her eyes, surprised by his tempting invitation. Breakfast with Ryan would kill any chance she'd have of making it to tennis this afternoon. But if her workload today grew any bigger, she'd have to stay back and miss tennis even if she started work half an hour early.

His eyes twinkled. "I can recommend their bacon and eggs."

Her stomach rumbled. She'd need to eat something substantial soon. "A muffin and fruit salad would hit the spot."

"That will work." He lounged back in his seat, a satisfied expression on his face.

Her gaze roamed over the familiar landmarks as the ferry glided toward the quay. Rays of sunlight beamed through the windows although the sky remained gray, highlighting the stark whiteness of the Sydney Opera House. The ferry docked and they were soon on their way to breakfast.

Ryan chose an indoor table at the café and pulled out a wooden chair for her. A waiter came straight over to take their order, scribbled down their choices, then returned to the kitchen.

Ryan sat opposite her, his hands clasped together on the table and a distant look lingering in his eyes.

She searched his face, unable to read his thoughts. Why did he look so serious? Had she done something wrong?

"How was your weekend?" he asked, switching his attention back to her.

"Pretty good. Did you visit your parents?"

He nodded. "I'm glad I did. Another debt collector turned up on their doorstep looking for Sean."

"What happened?"

"We found out he'd applied for credit cards in Melbourne a few months ago. He blew the limits straight away and did a runner."

"That's terrible. How did your parents take the news?"

"Not well. They're both really stressed."

"Where's Sean?"

"We don't know." He raked his hand through his hair. "Do you remember his friend Billy?"

She nodded.

"He works next door to me and he's certain he saw Sean at Bondi Beach a few weeks ago."

Her jaw dropped. "Sean's in Sydney?"

"We think so."

Apprehension shot through her, and their last meeting before he'd disappeared flashed into her mind. What would she do if she saw him again?

Her immediate answers weren't pleasant, but the likelihood of running into him couldn't be huge in a city as big as Sydney.

The waiter returned with their breakfast and Ryan devoured his bacon and eggs. When did he find the time to maintain his athletic physique?

She picked at her fruit salad. "Do you think you'll find him soon?"

"He'll eventually run out of money and I doubt he's foolish enough to contact me or my parents."

"Why? Wouldn't he realize you could help him?"

"My brother's looking for money, not help. He'll go to extreme lengths to get what he wants. You're an easy target. He may contact you."

Cassie gasped. "Are you saying I'm a pushover?"

"He'll use anyone to get money." Concern softened his eyes. "Does he owe you money?"

She shook her head, alarmed that Sean might seek her out after all this time.

"Then you'll be on his hit list."

No way! This couldn't be happening. Her head started to ache. "You really think he'll come looking for me?"

He nodded. "I don't want to see you hurt."

Cassie shivered. Would Sean try to hurt her again? She hoped and prayed Ryan was wrong.

Chapter 3

Cassie perused the contents of her mother's fridge, locating the springwater at the back. The rich chocolate dessert her mom had made for their Thursday night family dinner caught her attention.

Her taste buds tingled. A small serving of dessert tonight would satisfy her sweet tooth. This afternoon she'd done her final bridesmaid fitting with Laura, and the striking blue silk dress inspired her to eat healthy. She'd been on edge during the fitting, knowing the boutique was only a few suburbs away from where Sean had been sighted.

Cassie frowned. Over the past few days she'd been looking over her shoulder and scrutinizing the faces of strangers walking past. Ryan's warning played over again in her mind. Would Sean really harass her for money? Was he lurking nearby?

Determined to enjoy a pleasant dinner with her mom and sister, she cast aside her worries. She'd work out how to deal with Sean later if he turned up.

She poured a glass of water and wandered outside to join her mom. The wafting aroma of barbecuing chicken brought a smile to her lips. "This smells great."

Susan spun around on two-inch heels and adjusted her apron over her designer jeans and sweater. "I'm using a recipe from that nice-looking chef on the Lifestyle channel."

"Mom, he's younger than me."

"So what?" Her blue eyes sparkled. "Great cooking is near the top of my perfect man list."

She pressed her lips together, refusing to debate the merits of her mom's dubious list and not wanting to hear any more stories about her father's lousy cooking.

Susan raised a manicured brow. "Where's Laura?"

"Upstairs in her room. Greg's stuck at work and she called him as we came in. Do you want me to make a salad?"

She shook her head. "I'll fix it and let the chicken sizzle a little longer. Has she found a dress?"

Cassie rolled her eyes. "Not yet. She's looked at heaps of dresses but can't decide which designer she wants, let alone the style."

"She'd better hurry and make up her mind."

"We're going shopping again in a few weeks and she promised me she'd make a decision by then."

"I hope so." She ran her fingers through her short blond curls. "Why don't you go back indoors where it's warm and I'll be in soon?"

Cassie nodded and returned to the living room. She pulled out a chair at the wooden table overlooking the kitchen and outdoor courtyard.

Susan came inside and rinsed some lettuce leaves in the sink. "Have you spoken to your father?"

"Not since the weekend."

"I thought you were going to call him this week."

A decision she'd made before the party, when she'd been deluded and actually believed he'd appreciate her hard work. "He knows my number if he wants to talk to me."

Her mom drained the leaves before adding them to a white ceramic bowl with the other ingredients. "You're still angry with him over the party?"

She nodded. "He thinks Laura should have hired a professional party planner."

"But he knew Laura wanted you to organize it."

"Apparently I'm not good enough for him, even though the party was a big success. He didn't say thank-you or anything."

Susan frowned. "You know he's hopeless at talking about his feelings."

"That's not the point."

"You've got to keep trying."

"We always end up arguing." She dropped her gaze. "I'm glad Laura gets on with him, but it's different for me."

"Maybe, but your father cares about you and wants what's best for you."

"Yeah, and that's why he's always critical and thinks I make stupid decisions? Just because he was right about Sean doesn't mean he always knows best."

"Maybe you need to talk to him about Sean."

Cassie shook her head. "Not after the massive fight we had two years ago."

"Are you sure?"

"I want to make things better, not worse." She wanted to fix their relationship, but so much had happened…

"He probably thought he was helping you by telling you about Sean."

"Maybe, but he should have realized I'd be hurt and angry." She blinked away a few tears that threatened to escape between her lashes.

"I wish you'd talked to me. I could have helped you."

"You couldn't have done anything." She met her mom's concerned gaze. "My faith has helped me."

Susan's frown deepened. "I don't understand your religious nonsense, but I guess it's good that you think it's helping you."

Cassie tightened her grip on her glass. Now was not the time to get into another heated discussion.

Susan carried the salad bowl over to the table and sat beside her. "One day you'll have to deal with these problems."

She closed her eyes and took a deep breath. Mom's attitude toward her father had softened in recent weeks. Maybe Laura's upcoming wedding had something to do with her mom's sudden change of heart.

Footsteps thumped down the stairs. She opened her eyes and Laura breezed into the room.

"Something smells good. Is dinner ready yet?"

Susan stood. "The chicken should be done. I'll be back soon."

Laura sat down opposite Cassie. "So, what's the deal with you and Ryan?"

"He's nice."

"Is that all you can say?" She ran her fingers through her brunette locks. "You two looked cozy last weekend and I waited all afternoon for you to tell me what's going on."

She sighed. Laura would probe her for information until she cracked. "It's no big deal. We caught the same ferry the other day and we're going sailing on Sunday."

Laura grinned. "I knew it. You two are perfect for each other."

"I'm not so sure. Give me a chance to get to know him first before you start planning another wedding."

"You must like him a lot to be seeing him Sunday."

"We're friends and I haven't been out sailing in ages."

"You'll have a fantastic time. He's interested in you and before long you'll be more than friends."

Cassie let her comment slide. Her sister needed no further encouragement in her matchmaking.

Their mom returned with the chicken and they helped her serve dinner.

Cassie broke apart a warm roll and smiled. It was good to catch up with her family.

"This chicken is beautiful," Laura said.

Cassie sampled a bite. "I'll have to add the recipe to my collection."

Susan laughed. "You mean lose it in your collection."

She shot her mom a stern look. "One day I'll find time to organize my recipes."

"So you keep saying."

Laura smiled. "Speaking of organizing things, I haven't told you my news yet."

Cassie lifted a brow. What was her sister up to now?

"Greg just confirmed that his parents' holiday house in the Blue Mountains will be free on the weekend I've chosen." Her smile widened. "Isn't that excellent?"

"Sure." Cassie dropped her gaze. *Miss Matchmaker strikes again.* Laura wanted her bridal party to get together before the wedding. In theory a good idea. But why did it have to involve a whole weekend away with two couples and Ryan? An uncomfortable situation would arise if she and Ryan had a falling out, but she couldn't see a way to change Laura's mind.

Susan smiled. "You have it all organized?"

Laura nodded. "Anna and Craig can definitely make it. I haven't spoken to Ryan yet, but Greg said he's due back from Melbourne tomorrow."

Cassie swallowed hard, resisting the urge to ask her sister about Ryan's schedule. She prayed she'd made the right decision to see him on Sunday.

Cassie pulled her hair back into a ponytail and layered clear gloss on her lips. She checked her watch. Ryan was due to arrive any minute.

Her stomach churned as she slung her backpack over her shoulder and headed into the living room of her apartment.

Her roommate, Julia, looked up from the sofa and smiled, closing the book in her lap. "You'll have a great time sailing."

"I hope so, but I'm nervous."

Julia's green eyes widened. "You must really like him."

She nibbled her lower lip, tasting the strawberry flavor of her gloss. "At first I was skeptical because of Sean, but now…"

"Don't stress and just enjoy getting to know Ryan better."

Before she could relax she needed to share her niggling concerns. "I'm going to level with you." She examined her fingernails. "I don't know if Ryan's a believer."

Julia stood, tucking her dark auburn locks behind her ears. "You can still be friends and maybe invite him to church."

"You think that's a good idea?" She shifted her weight from one foot to the other.

"He's seen you reading the Bible and probably assumes you go to church."

She nodded.

"And he didn't cancel seeing you today. That must mean something."

"Yeah, but what?"

"I don't know. Maybe you could ask him today."

Her heart sank. What if she didn't get the answer she wanted?

"I'll be praying," Julia said.

"Thanks." She gave her best friend a brief hug before closing her apartment door and racing down the stairs two at a time. *Lord, please help me to make wise decisions.*

Cassie stepped outside and slipped on her sunglasses. Ryan drove along the street and stopped in her drive. She opened the passenger door, made herself comfortable in the front seat and flashed him a big smile.

His gray eyes sparkled. "Good to see you're all set and ready to go."

She nodded. "I can't wait to get out on the water."

"Me, too." He put his sunglasses on and swung the SUV onto the street.

He seemed relaxed and looked good in his casual blue sweater and cargo pants.

She stared out the window, unable to ignore the tension clenching her heart. Unanswered questions flitted through her mind.

Julia was right. If the subject didn't come up earlier, she could mention her faith during their drive home later today and invite him to church this evening if he seemed interested.

Before long Ryan pulled into a parking bay in a leafy street above the yacht club.

Jacaranda branches swayed overhead in the cloudless sky. She unbuckled her seat belt. "The wind's picking up."

He nodded. "We'll only need to motor in and out of the bay. I could use your help with the mainsail."

Distant memories of assisting her father on his yacht sprang to mind. "I haven't done any real sailing in ages."

"Once we're out on the water you'll remember everything."

She hoped so, not that she had much knowledge to recall. Lying back on the deck had been more her style.

Ryan collected his gear from the back of his SUV before walking with her on the path leading down to the yacht club.

She inhaled the salty air carried by the breeze and swiped her ponytail back off her face. Her cable-knit sweater and comfortable jeans kept her warm.

Pausing on the steps, she drank in the beauty of the bay. A quaint wooden clubhouse overlooked the shimmering water with a vast array of boating craft moored around it.

He stopped beside her. "We're not the only ones taking advantage of the good weather."

"On sunny days like today you can forget it's still winter." She continued walking with him along the path toward the busy clubhouse.

Ryan retrieved his dinghy from a nearby shed and dropped it in the water next to the dock.

He leapt into the dinghy, displaying excellent balance as it bobbed about underneath him.

She helped him load their gear and then he held out his hand.

"Thanks." She stepped down into the dinghy, her hand trembling within his firm grasp.

She sucked in a deep breath and scurried onto the bench opposite him. Her intense awareness of him had knocked her off balance.

He grabbed hold of the oars and began rowing out into the bay.

She studied the assortment of yachts surrounding them before they pulled up beside a yacht named Adventurer.

"Ready?" He steadied the dinghy for her.

Cassie nodded and leapt onto the deck. Her gaze roamed over the yacht, taking in the state-of-the-art fixtures and navigation equipment. No expense had been spared.

After unloading the last of their gear, Ryan tied the dinghy to the stern of the yacht. He unlocked the hatch, lifted up the solid cover and started checking the equipment.

She shifted their gear down into the cabin, eyeing the picnic hamper and cooler bag. What had he brought for lunch?

The engine roared to life as she climbed back on the deck.

He smiled. "Are you ready to help me with the mainsail?"

"Yep." She followed behind him, admiring his agility as he clamored over the deck and ducked under the boom.

Her sense of balance returned, giving her the confidence to loosen her grip on the side railing.

He untied the main halyard and handed it to her.

She grabbed hold of it, looking up at where it disappeared into the top of the mast. "When do you want me to pull on the rope?"

"Now," he said.

She followed his instructions, maintaining a firm grip on the halyard while he set the sail into the right position. The stark white sail billowed in the breeze as they worked together to secure the lines to hold it in place.

"Sailing is so random," she said. "Name another sport where you begin miles behind the starting line and then hope you don't pass through it before the starter sounds."

He shrugged. "It's all part of the challenge, plus choosing the right wind to follow."

"Too many variables for my liking."

"Then you're better off sticking with a more precise sport like tennis."

She lifted a brow. "How do you know I play tennis?"

"Laura suggested we play doubles with her and Greg sometime."

She cringed. Did her sister's matchmaking have to be so obvious? What else had she said to him?

Ryan raised the anchor and steered the yacht out of the bay before shutting down the engine. He stood tall behind the helm, looking at ease and in control of his world.

She lounged back on a cushioned bench seat in the cockpit and absorbed the peaceful atmosphere of the bay. Majestic homes scattered between low-rise apartment buildings lined the foreshores. Seagulls skirted over the gentle waves, looking for an early lunch.

She tightened her ponytail and secured her baseball cap in place. "What's the plan for today?"

"We'll tack down the harbor toward Manly." He adjusted his sunglasses on the bridge of his nose.

"How rough will it be?"

"Not too rough." His smile widened. "I'll steer clear of the ferries."

"I sure hope that won't be a problem."

He laughed. "I don't take risks with my baby."

"Good."

"But don't get too comfortable in your seat."

"I know." She stretched out her legs. "I'm ready to switch sides when you give the word."

He nodded. "Ready about."

Cassie jumped across to the bench seat on the other side of the cockpit. The sharp angle of the yacht required her to brace her body in an almost upright position, balancing her feet on the opposite bench seat.

Ryan shifted the yacht around onto the next tack. The boom flew over the front deck to the other side of the boat. The yacht gained speed and continued its zigzag route down the harbor.

Each time the yacht tacked she switched sides to avoid sliding backwards, headfirst, into the water.

At least in the cockpit she didn't need to duck under the swinging boom. Waves started to lap over the bow of the yacht as it cruised through the building swell near the entrance to the harbor.

She tightened her grip on the handles as they tacked toward the open sea. The yacht traveled through the turbulent ocean at breathtaking speed.

"How are you doing?" he asked.

"Fine," she said. "I'd forgotten how fun this can be."

"The wind's good." He yanked his cap lower over his face. "Strong enough to give us speed but not too strong that we end up drenched."

"That's okay. I brought a change of clothes just in case."

He grinned. "We should reach our lunch destination soon."

Before long a small cove with a beach surrounded by native bush came into view.

"We can ride the tide to this cove where we'll drop anchor for lunch, if that suits you?"

She nodded. "All this hopping around has given me an appetite."

"I'm glad to hear it, because we have a feast awaiting us."

"I'm impressed you've organized lunch."

"A gutsy decision, considering you're a catering expert."

"But not a critical one."

"Then I'm a lucky man. I throw people overboard who complain about the food."

She giggled. "I'll keep that in mind. It's a shame I can't throw clients out the window who complain at the hotel."

He laughed. "Remind me not to get on your bad side in high-rise buildings."

"I'm really a sweet girl at heart, but I've been told I've inherited my father's tenacity."

"Your poor mother. How did she cope?"

"She gained a few gray hairs, not that she'd ever admit it."

"Smart lady. We met briefly at the party."

Cassie smiled. "You made quite an impression on her."

"A favorable one, I hope."

She nodded, remembering her mom's glowing remarks.

He steered the yacht into the cove and dropped anchor.

"Can I help with lunch?"

He shook his head. "I'll fix it now. You can relax and I'll be back soon." He disappeared into the cabin below.

Gentle waves lapped over the sandy beach in the small cove, and a group of children played in the shallows. Half a dozen boats were moored around the cove.

She stretched out on the warm deck. If only she could spend more of her weekends cruising around the harbor with Ryan.

He emerged from the cabin and set up the foldaway table between the bench seats. She struggled up from her prone position on the deck and sat under the boom awning.

"I was beginning to think I'd lost you for the afternoon," he said.

"Hunger pangs would have shifted me." A selection of salads, fruit and bread filled the table. "This looks delicious."

"I raided the gourmet deli this morning."

She slipped into a seat opposite Ryan and he served her a plate of nutritious goodies.

They chatted through lunch and she still didn't have any answers concerning his faith. She could say something now, but why rush? They could talk later.

Before long he'd devoured his plate of food and she finished eating a crunchy red apple.

She stretched her arms out above her head, stifling a yawn. "You organized lunch so I'll start cleaning up."

"Let me do it."

"I'm happy to help."

"There's not much to do." He gathered up the leftovers and took them below deck.

Heavy-eyed from the warm sun and a full stomach, she shaped her towel into a pillow on the shady side of the deck. She closed her eyes for a moment and inhaled the refreshing sea air. How easy it would be to fall asleep.

A shuffling noise lured her out of her restful state. She sat up, rubbing her eyes.

"Did you have a nice nap?" Ryan asked.

"I'm sorry I dropped off."

"No problem." He sat beside her and reached for her hand. "I've had maintenance stuff to do."

Cassie looked up and his smoldering gray eyes captured her gaze.

He raised his other hand, skimming his tapered fingers over her cheek. Warmth radiated from him as he lowered his head toward her.

She closed her eyes and parted her lips, welcoming his featherlight caress. Her mouth tingled and she twined her fingers in his windswept hair. Tilting her head up, she drew his mouth back to hers.

He cupped her face with his hands and released her lips, his gaze searching her eyes.

She smiled. *Wow.* She drew in a deep breath to try to calm her racing thoughts.

"Cassie, you're one amazing woman."

She lowered her lashes, the logical part of her brain starting to tick over. What was she doing, kissing Ryan before she had determined if she wanted a relationship with him to go somewhere? Had she learned nothing from her past mistakes?

She traced her tongue over her upper lip, longing to kiss him again and rekindle their magnetic connection. But first she needed answers to the questions she'd put off asking all day.

"Do you have plans for tonight?"

"Not yet."

She stared into the warm depths of his eyes. "I was wondering if you'd like to come to church with me."

His eyes widened, remaining fixed on her. "I haven't been to church in ages." He paused for a few seconds. "Why not?"

Chapter 4

On Sunday evening Ryan sat in a cushioned plastic chair beside Cassie at Beachside Community Church.

Cassie whispered in his ear. "The service should start any minute."

"Okay." The subtle scent of her perfume brought a smile to his lips.

The church was located in a historic sandstone building with a modernized interior. A group of singers and musicians belted out contemporary music from a large stage at the front.

Not the type of music for quiet contemplation and nothing like the somber hymns from his church back home. Did they use the pipe organ at the front of the sanctuary? Or have a choir?

A singer introduced the opening song and he stood with the congregation.

Cassie leaned closer. "What do you think?"

"It's different."

She smiled. "I like it here."

Why? What attracted her to this church? "I'm used to a more traditional church."

"We have a traditional service in the morning."

He nodded, unable to envision his parents enjoying this style of worship. "Do you go in the morning?"

"Sometimes."

His childhood experiences at a small church in the country hadn't prepared him for the intensity of this vibrant church community. Encouraged by his parents, he attended services at Christmas and Easter. He complied more out of duty than a desire to learn about God.

He believed in God, figured he was doing okay and would end up in heaven one day.

The second song commenced and Cassie's face lit up, her body swaying in beat with the music.

Standing still, he fixed his gaze on the overhead screen. Why were all these people excited about being in church? It didn't make sense. His idea of God was a distant man in the sky who wouldn't approve of his people having fun!

"Are you okay?" she asked. "You look a bit shell-shocked."

"It's not what I expected, but I'm glad I'm here with you." Her presence made up for his discomfort.

She squeezed his hand. "So am I."

He held her hand, not wanting to break their connection. Vivid memories of their kiss earlier that day lingered in his mind. He didn't regret his impulsive urge to kiss her, and he'd do it again if the opportunity arose.

Cassie inspired thoughts in him of settling down. But their relationship would become complicated after he found Sean.

His brother couldn't hide forever. He'd heard another rumor that he'd been spotted at an inner-city café.

Maybe he should hire a private investigator. He refused to watch another Christmas pass with his mother shedding tears for her lost son.

Before long the pastor stood on the stage and began his sermon.

Ryan sat still, fascinated by the pastor's words. Did God really want to have a personal relationship with him? Wouldn't God be too busy running the universe to be concerned with him?

He stood for the closing songs. Something had shifted

in his world and for the first time in years he considered how God fitted into his life. He couldn't remember the last time he'd prayed or thought about God.

The service ended and Cassie turned to face him. "I usually have coffee in the hall next door. Would you like to join me?"

He smiled. "Sure. Coffee sounds good."

"Was the service very different from what you're used to?"

"Yeah, but the sermon was interesting."

She nodded. "I find Simon's sermons helpful. He's heading our way."

He turned to find a young, energetic man waving in their direction. Simon didn't look old enough to be a pastor. At his old church, the pastors usually had gray hair and grandchildren.

Cassie made the introductions and someone yelled out her name from across the aisle.

"I'll be back in a minute," she said.

"No worries," Ryan said.

Simon smiled. "So you're a friend of Cassie's?"

"I also work for her father, and her sister's engaged to one of my friends."

"That's right. I recently met Greg and Laura and I'll be officiating at their ceremony."

He nodded. Simon was the cool preacher guy Greg had talked about last week. "I guess you do lots of weddings."

"Yes, but I have every third Saturday off to spend with my wife and baby girl."

"I assume Sunday is always a workday for you."

"True, but I love my job and I can't imagine doing anything else. I studied to be a lawyer and worked in a law firm for a few years before going to Bible college."

"An interesting decision."

Simon grinned. "The right decision for me."

A teenage boy approached Simon. "Jack said to tell you Hannah's ready now."

"Ryan, it's been great talking with you and I hope we'll see you again."

He shook Simon's hand. "Sure. See you later."

Simon followed the teenage boy down the middle aisle toward the front of the church.

Ryan searched the crowd for Cassie. Why would someone like Simon turn his back on a lucrative career in law?

Cassie appeared by his side.

"Ryan, I'm sorry that took so long. Did you have a chance to talk to Simon?"

He nodded. "He seems content with his life as a pastor."

"He's good at his job. By the way, are you in Sydney all week?"

"Yes, I've got a ton of work to get through." He paused. "The company-sponsored charity dinner is on Friday night. Are you going?"

Her eyes widened. "I'd forgotten all about it. Laura mentioned it ages ago and Dad will expect me to be there."

"Would you like to come with me? I've got two tickets and I was hoping to see you next weekend." He leaned back, resting his hands on the row of seats behind him.

"Okay." She twisted a lock of hair around her finger. "Dad would be ticked off if I didn't make an appearance."

"Great." He tightened his grip on the chairs. "I'll pick you up from your place at six."

Did she want to attend the dinner with him? Or did she agree to go because she wanted to appease her father? A few days ago her father had asked him if he'd invited Cassie to the dinner.

The church building emptied out. "Did you say there was coffee nearby?"

"I'll lead the way," she said.

He walked beside her to the hall. After greeting a number of people he realized he wouldn't mind coming back again.

* * *

The security intercom buzzed on Friday evening and Cassie stashed her makeup in the bathroom cabinet. Ryan was five minutes early.

The buzzer sounded again. She padded barefoot across her carpeted living room and picked up the intercom handset.

"Hey, Cassie, are you ready?" Ryan asked.

Butterflies skittered in her belly. "Nearly. Come on up."

She left her front door ajar and retreated to her bedroom. She slipped on her flimsy black sandals and caught a glimpse of her reflection in the full-length mirror.

Her black fitted dress glided over her curves. Delicate spaghetti straps held the straight bodice in place and the full length skirt swirled around her ankles.

She rummaged through her antique jewelry box, locating her sapphire and diamond pendant. Lifting up her hair, she attached the necklace given to her by her paternal grandmother.

Lord, please help me to resist temptation tonight. Help me to remember that even one tiny sip will cause me grief.

She sprayed her favorite floral scent and heard the front door close.

A shiver of anticipation coursed through her as she left the sanctuary of her bedroom. She found Ryan in her living room, studying the framed photographs on the side table next to the sofa.

Her breath caught in her throat. His tailored pin-striped suit added to his aura of authority and emphasized his athletic build.

"Ryan, I'm ready."

"Great." He smiled, an ornate silver frame cradled in the palm of his hand.

"A happy family snap from long ago."

"Your dad looks different with lots of hair."

"He wore it long when we were kids, and Mom used to

tease him about having hair longer than her own." Her parents looked happy together in the photo. Why did her father have to run off with another woman and ruin everything?

Ryan held her gaze, his smile widening. "You look incredible. I like your hair loose."

Her face heated and she unclenched her moist palms, sucking in a steadying breath. "Thanks, this dress is one of my favorites. Would you like a drink before we go?"

He shook his head. "We need to get moving, beautiful lady."

He placed the photo frame back on the side table, hooked his arm through hers and escorted her out of her apartment.

The chill in the evening air took her by surprise and she pulled her wrap closer around her shoulders.

He slowed his stride, falling into step beside her.

They reached his SUV and he opened the passenger door.

The soft leather seat molded to fit the shape of her body and she felt like Cinderella heading to the ball, but without a disaster ready to strike at midnight.

Ryan hopped in beside her and revved the engine to life. He maneuvered the vehicle through the backstreets and onto the main road leading to the city. Music from a local radio station played in the background.

Her appearance at the dinner tonight would please her father. To get past her issues with his behavior at the engagement party, she needed to let go of her hurt and forgive him. In theory a good idea but much easier said than done.

Dad approved of Ryan. Dating Ryan might help her relationship with Dad, but her niggling doubts remained. Was she making a mistake?

The traffic crawled along and Cassie appreciated the blast of heating. The warmer spring weather was still a few weeks away.

The heat and humidity of North Queensland would be a welcome change. Yesterday she had received notification of her success in the first round for the job in Queensland. In the next few weeks she hoped to confirm a date and flight details for an interview at the resort.

Ryan seemed deep in thought. She could mention her upcoming job interview. What would he think? Would he tell her father?

Dad would be furious if he found out her news through someone else, and she wasn't ready to broach the subject with him.

Lord, please help me to have a fruitful conversation with Dad. I'm sick of the arguments. Help us to rebuild our relationship tonight.

She played with the clasp on her purse. "How many people will be at the dinner?"

"A couple hundred. I've arranged for us to sit with Laura and Greg."

"Good." At least she'd know someone at their table. She hadn't visited her father at work or attended many company-related functions since Sean had left.

The traffic flowed steadily over the harbor bridge. He turned off at the first exit and within minutes the hotel towered up ahead.

The hotel lobby hummed with activity. Ryan placed his hand over her elbow and guided her to the ballroom.

Cassie searched the crowd for her sister. "Have you seen Laura?"

He shook his head. "Let's go inside and find her."

He escorted her into the ballroom. A spectacular chandelier hung from the elaborate ceiling. Dozens of round tables, covered by crisp white linen tablecloths, filled the spacious room. The guests congregated near the bar, sipping predinner drinks.

"They've done a fabulous job with the decorations," she said. "I wonder who does their floral arrangements."

"Hey, you're a guest, remember." He stopped beside her. "Time to relax and forget about work."

"Occupational hazard, I'm afraid. There's Laura." She spotted her sister in a flamboyant red dress.

She walked ahead and greeted her.

"Ryan, you look dashing tonight," Laura said.

"So do you." He smiled. "Where's Greg?"

Laura rolled her eyes. "Mingling somewhere."

He turned to Cassie. "I need to talk with a few clients. I'll leave you two to chat and be back soon."

"No problem," Cassie said.

Laura gave Ryan a conspiratorial wink. "Cassie and I have some catching up to do."

Cassie smiled. "Take your time and we'll meet you at our table."

"Okay." Ryan disappeared into the crowd.

Laura took hold of her arm. "You must tell me everything."

"There isn't much to tell."

"I'm not blind. I can see those warm looks passing between you two."

"This is only our second date, well actually our third if you count breakfast the other week. It's early days."

Laura embraced her in a big hug. "You're falling for him. I knew it would happen because you two are perfect for each other. I'm so excited."

"You're getting ahead of yourself. There's no rush. Give us time to get to know each other."

"Of course. I've done my job in prodding you both in the right direction. Dad will be pleased."

Cassie lifted a brow. "What's Dad got to do with this?"

"Ryan and Greg are his two top executives. He'll be delighted if they both became his sons-in-law."

Cassie clenched her fist, digging her nails into her palm. "Did Dad put you up to this?"

Hurt flared in her sister's eyes. "Absolutely not, but it's about time you both reconciled your differences. I see your dating Ryan as a positive step in that direction."

She drew in a calming breath. Her father could be dictatorial, but accusing him of interfering in her love life…

Laura frowned. "Please don't be mad at me."

"Has Dad said something to you? Did Dad tell Ryan to date me?"

"He's aware you're seeing Ryan and he approves. I've no idea what he's said to Ryan, but I thought you'd be happy about this. You keep telling me you want to fix your relationship with Dad."

"I'm sorry. I know you'd never intentionally do anything to hurt me."

"You're forgiven." Laura hugged her again. "But I can't help seeing the benefits for your relationship with Dad if you date someone he approves of. After the fiasco of your friendship with Sean…"

"I know." She stared at the plush carpeted floor. "Hanging out with Sean wasn't the smartest decision I ever made. But I'm a different person now, and I'm trying to do the right thing."

"I'm so proud of you. It's unfortunate you got caught up in Sean's mess, but it's unlikely he'll return anytime soon. Now, let's find our table so we can start on the appetizers that are being served."

Cassie took her seat next to Laura, inhaling the spicy aroma of the Thai beef salad in front of her.

She tasted the beef and smiled. Cooked to perfection. Her father would be pleased the food was top-notch.

Ryan slipped into the seat beside her. "How's it going?"

"Good. I haven't seen Dad yet."

"He's caught up with some clients and he said he'll drop by our table when he's done."

Cassie sipped her iced water. "Thanks for letting me know."

"No problem. I've done all the mingling I need to do so you have my undivided attention."

Ryan's warm gaze created havoc with her composure.

If only she could stare into his eyes all night and ignore everything else going on around her.

Their appetizers were promptly cleared away and replaced by an Atlantic salmon entrée.

She tilted her head sideways. "I'm really glad I came with you tonight."

"So am I." His eyes sparkled. "I wish it was just the two of us."

Her heart skipped a beat. Maybe they could duck away early and take a moonlit walk by the water.

Her gaze swept over the ballroom. At least three hundred people filled the room. A number of celebrities had shown up to lend their support. "The Children's Hospital needs the money raised here tonight."

"It's a full house and your father is happy with the turnout."

Cassie sampled the salmon, wondering when her father would swing by their table.

Before long she placed her napkin next to her empty plate, deciding it was time to freshen up her makeup.

She stood, excusing herself to go to the restroom. "I won't be long."

"I'll be here waiting for you." His gray eyes softened and matched the warmth in his deep voice.

"I'll be quick." She tore her gaze from him and walked away from the table.

Wow. Ryan's warm looks sent her senses into overdrive.

She weaved her way across the room and turned into the hall leading to the restrooms.

A man stepped out in front of her, blocking her path. She looked up and gasped. "Sean."

Chapter 5

Sean smiled. "Cassie."

Cassie opened her mouth but no words came out. What was he doing here?

"Aren't you going to say hello? Or give me a welcome-home hug?"

Covering her mouth with both hands, she stepped away from him.

How long had he been here? Dressed in a charcoal business suit and sporting a conservative haircut, he'd easily blend in with the other guests at the dinner.

His gaze swept down the length of her. "You're looking good."

"What do you want?"

His smile widened. "To see you, of course."

Her anger ascended to the surface. "How dare you?"

"Now don't go and get upset on me—"

"Don't patronize me." She thrust her hands on her hips. "What do you think you're doing?"

His eyes narrowed. "Can't we have a civilized conversation?"

"There's nothing civilized about the way you left. The word *callous* comes to mind."

"I want to talk to you about that."

"That's right—you've had two years to think up a good excuse for why you took off."

"You don't understand—"

"I understand all too well." She took a step forward. "Please move out of my way."

He held his ground. "I heard you're dating my brother. He'll lose interest in you now I've returned."

She ignored his gibe, flattening her palms against the side of her dress to keep her fists from hammering his conceited face.

"I've been thinking about how much fun we used to have together." He slid his arm around her shoulder. "We should get together sometime—"

"Get away from me." She wrenched out of his hold, his touch sending a chill through her body.

She spun on her heel and ran the five remaining steps to the ladies' room. The door closed behind her and she leaned back against it, breathing hard.

Hot tears filled her eyes. Sean's arrogance stunned her. Her sobriety gave her a clearer picture of his true nature.

She staggered over to the washbasins, grimacing at her reflection in the mirror.

Footsteps sounded outside the door. She rushed over to a cubicle and locked herself in, needing time to pull herself together.

Tinkling laughter from the girls who entered the ladies' room jarred her overwrought nerves. Hopefully they didn't intend to hang around for long.

"My lipstick's smudged already."

"My hair isn't sitting right. I should have used more mousse."

"Girls, did you notice Ryan Mitchell is here?"

Cassie's back stiffened against the wall of the cubicle.

"Who didn't?"

"He's cute and rich. What I wouldn't give for a night on the town with him…."

"Isn't he here with some blonde?"

"His boss's daughter," a new voice piped in.

Cassie bit hard on her lower lip.

"Could be a business arrangement."

"He'd do well financially if he married her."

"I heard she's a bit of an ice maiden these days. A church girl, if the rumors are true."

"Really." A high-pitched giggle floated across the room. "He'll soon be bored with her, and I'll be there waiting for him when he slips through her fingers."

"No way! I saw him first."

"If he prefers blondes you won't have a chance."

"Now girls, hold back the claws. I heard James is back on the market."

"He dumped Kelly already? Let's find him and cheer him up."

Their footsteps finally receded and the restroom door clicked behind them.

Cassie buried her face in her hands. Those girls had a nerve. Their cruel gossip had ripped apart her old wounds and resurrected her insecurities.

She should ignore their idle talk. No longer did she seek to be popular and liked by everyone. While she valued the opinions of the important people in her life, it was God's approval that mattered.

She cared about Ryan. The prospect of a serious relationship with him had filled her thoughts since their sailing date.

Now her initial doubts resurfaced. Was Ryan seeing her because of her father? Was money a motive? Would he dump her as soon as he found out Sean had returned?

Fury at Sean's behavior ripped through her. She tightened her grip on her purse, her muscles tensing as she suppressed the urge to scream at the top of her lungs.

How could Sean reappear as if nothing had happened? He'd hurt so many people.

He'd hurt her. She'd drunk herself into oblivion to numb the pain. Her father's harsh words rang in her mind. Their arguments over Sean had pushed her to rock bottom.

Two years later she still fought the desire to drink away the memories and dull the emotions bubbling inside her.

An icy chill engulfed her. *What will Ryan do when he sees Sean again?*

Lord, please help me to calm my anger so I can think rationally about Sean. I need every ounce of self-control I possess to stop myself beating him up. I know I should let go of my anger, but I can't. It's too hard. Please help Ryan to deal with his brother's return.

Cassie sucked in a deep breath and released the air from her lungs. What was the right course of action to take regarding Sean?

No answers were forthcoming and she wished Julia was here to give her some words of wisdom.

She unlocked the cubicle door and glanced at her reflection in the mirror above the washbasins. Rummaging through her purse, she found the necessary makeup to conceal the dark smudges under her eyes. If only she'd worn waterproof mascara tonight. She reapplied her lipstick, preparing to face the outside world.

She held her head high and strolled out of the ladies' room.

Sean stood in the hall and stepped toward her.

Her heart sank. *Not again.* Why couldn't he leave her alone?

"Cassie, please, I need to talk to you."

She narrowed her eyes. "Why?"

"I need to ask you a favor—"

"You must be kidding. After everything that's happened, you expect me to help you."

"I'm sorry about earlier. My behavior was out of line and I promise it won't happen again."

Did Sean's promises mean anything these days? She read the desperation in his eyes. "You have one minute."

"I need to talk to Ryan and I don't have a ticket to the dinner. Can you ask him to meet me in the lobby?"

"Contact Ryan yourself. It's not like he's hard to find."

"He's here, I'm here. I must see him tonight."

She planted her hands on her hips and looked him straight in the eye. "Why should I help you?"

"Because you're a nice person—"

"Right now I'm not thinking nice thoughts about you."

He raised his hands. "Cassie, I beg you. I need to see Ryan tonight."

"Do you really think he'll agree to see you?"

Sean paused. "Then don't tell him it's me."

"I'm not going to lie to him. Why don't you call him tomorrow?"

"Please, I'm begging you, this is important. I want to try and make amends with Ryan and explain my side of the story."

"This has nothing to do with me." She waved her hand through the air, dismissing his pleas. "I don't want to be involved and you need to sort this out with Ryan yourself."

"I know you care about Ryan. Wouldn't you like to see us reunited as a family?"

Family. Sean hit the right button, playing on her need to reconcile with her father. Did Sean realize his mother was grieving his absence, worried that something horrible had happened to him?

Knots of guilt over her own messy family situation wrenched her heart. How could she say no? "I'm not making any promises. Wait in the lobby."

"There's one more thing."

She lifted a brow. "You're in no position to negotiate more favors."

"You need to be there."

"In the lobby?"

He nodded.

"Why?"

"Ryan's more likely to give me a fair hearing if you're

there. Think of it as an investment in furthering good family relations."

She nibbled her lower lip. Maybe her presence would stop Ryan from thumping Sean. Not that she'd blame Ryan if the thought crossed his mind. "Okay."

"Thanks, Cassie." A broad smile covered his face. "You're the best!"

Yeah, right. She shot him a final terse look before heading back into the ballroom.

He'd aged since she'd last seen him. Fine lines surrounded his eyes and he looked like a man who'd seen tough times.

She walked toward the bar, her gaze homing in on a row of bottles. All her old favorites stood there, waiting for her.

A crowd gathered nearby. Would anyone notice if she knocked back a glass or two?

No. She had to be strong. Not even a sip.

Lord, please help me walk away now, before it's too late. Put one foot in front of the other and walk away from temptation. Think about something else.

Sean. The reason her thoughts had strayed to the bar. Where had he been for the past two years?

Cassie slipped into her seat beside Ryan. "I'm sorry I took so long."

"You've been gone for ages." He glanced at his watch. "Are you okay? You look flustered."

"You won't believe what's happened. He's here."

"Who's here?" Her father sat in the spare seat beside her.

"No one." Why did Dad have to turn up now? Talk about bad timing.

"Cassandra, what's going on?" her father asked.

"Nothing that concerns you."

Ryan frowned. "Something's wrong and you were gone a long time."

Dad shot her a sharp look. "Have you been drinking?"

"No, I told you I'm sober. Why can't you believe me?"

"Cassie, calm down." Ryan's gray eyes softened. "Tell me who's here."

She sucked in a soothing breath. Her father's accusation had pushed her too far. She counted to ten. The adrenaline rush started to subside.

She met Ryan's concerned gaze. "There's someone in the lobby waiting to see you."

Ryan raised an eyebrow. "Who is it?"

She chewed on her lower lip. What could she say? Her father would go berserk if he knew Sean was outside in the lobby. He'd probably call the police.

She leaned over and whispered in Ryan's ear. "I'll tell you when my father isn't in earshot."

Confusion clouded Ryan's face. "What's the problem? What are you hiding?"

"Well, Cassandra, isn't this convenient, arranging a mystery meeting for Ryan in the hotel lobby. If you didn't want to talk to me you should have just said so and I wouldn't have wasted my time stopping over to see you."

"Dad, you're wrong."

"I don't think so."

"Please believe me, Dad, this isn't my idea. Ryan can tell you all about it later." *Why now?* The perfect opportunity to talk to her father had been thwarted by Sean.

Her father stood. "Whatever. I'll be on my way."

"Dad, wait." Her father ignored her, striding away. She hadn't lost her talent for making things worse with him.

Ryan turned to face her. "Who is this mystery person?"

She grabbed hold of his hand. "Let's go to the lobby and get this over with."

Ryan walked beside Cassie in silence, the stony expression on her face worrying him.

He crossed the lobby to the lounge area. What had gotten into her? He'd never seen her lose control. The issues between father and daughter ran too deep for his liking.

He scanned the room and met a familiar pair of blue eyes. *Sean.* What was he doing here?

Sean offered him a bright smile. "Hey, big brother, how's things?"

Red-hot anger coursed through him, every muscle in his body tensing. "What are you playing at? Where have you been for the last two years?"

Sean raised his hands. "Take it easy, bro. I've been traveling, seeing the world—"

"Using the money you stole from Cassie's father. You think that's something to be proud of?"

"It was company money, and it's not like he's going to miss it."

"Do you think that makes it okay?" Cassie asked. "Fifty thousand dollars is a lot of money."

Ryan clenched his fists tighter. "I can't believe this. You have no remorse. I should have let John press charges against you."

Cassie frowned at Sean. "You do intend to make things right and repay the money, don't you?"

"Why bother?" Sean shrugged. "The company has probably already written off the loss."

"The company isn't out of pocket," he said.

Cassie arched an eyebrow. "Did Dad write it off?"

Ryan shook his head and glared at Sean. "I cleared the debt, so you owe me fifty thousand dollars."

Sean's mouth thinned into a grim line. "Why did you do that?"

"It was the right thing to do. Your actions put my career in a tenuous situation. John employed you in the first place under my recommendation so it became my responsibility to fix your mess."

"Well, you shouldn't have fixed it," Sean said.

What? Someone had to fix Sean's mess. He'd expected

him to be a little more grateful, since Sean would have ended up behind bars if Ryan hadn't intervened on his behalf.

Ryan took a deep breath. Now wasn't the time to lose it. "It's done, so now we can sit down and organize a payment plan. Have you spoken to Mom and Dad?"

Sean shook his head. "I will soon."

Yeah right. He'd heard that line before.

Sean shifted his weight from one foot to the other. "Money's a little tight at the moment. If we could postpone the payment plan for a few months—"

"No." Ryan stepped closer to Sean. "It's time you grew up and took responsibility for your actions. Let's settle this now."

"I feel bad about the money, but I've got a lot of expenses. If you've got a spare few hundred dollars I could borrow now, we could talk about a payment plan later."

"What? You expect me to lend you money?"

"I'm in a bind. Five hundred dollars would fix it—"

"No way! I'm not lending you a cent until you start repaying the money you already owe."

"We can talk about a payment plan next month. Right now I really need the extra cash."

"I get it. You have no intention of repaying me a cent of that money."

Sean stared at the floor and remained silent.

Ryan fumed. "Answer me now. Yes or no."

"I have to go." Sean passed a scrap of paper to Cassie. "My cell phone number. Call me."

"Wait up." Ryan stepped forward. "Don't you walk away from me."

Sean rushed out the main door, disappearing in the crowd on the street.

Ryan muttered a few choice words under his breath. *The next time I get my hands on him...*

Cassie's mouth gaped open and she stared at the slip of paper in her hand. "I can't believe he left, just like that."

"Sean hasn't changed."

"I guess not."

"I made a mistake in bailing him out, but it won't happen again. As far as I'm concerned he's nothing to me until he shows some remorse and starts repaying the money."

She nodded. "But you'll forgive him eventually?"

He shook his head. "Sean needs to do the right thing and repay the money before I can consider forgiving him. You've no idea the pain and suffering he has inflicted on my parents."

"I'll call him sometime. I need to sort out my issues with him so I can put all this stuff behind me."

"You do realize that he probably won't apologize. Do you want him harassing you for money?"

"Of course not. He may not give me an apology, but I can deal with it. I can still work on forgiving him so I can move on."

Ryan frowned. "Let me get this straight. You're going to forgive him even if he never says he's sorry?"

"It won't happen overnight, but life's too short to hold grudges over stuff like this."

How could she even consider letting him off the hook? "I disagree with you." He looked her straight in the eye. "But I'm too angry to talk about this now. I need to get out of here."

"I'll duck back inside and say our goodbyes."

He nodded. "I'll wait here."

He paced the length of the lobby, ignoring the strange looks from the other hotel guests. A workout with his punching bag would help release his aggravation. How dare Sean ask him for money?

The painful truth sank in. His brother didn't care about him. Sean would use him to get what he wanted, but that was it. Without hesitation, his brother had walked out on him and refused to make the situation right.

How could Cassie even entertain the idea of forgiving his ungrateful brother? During the drive home in the car he intended to convince her to change her mind. Otherwise, how would Sean ever learn to do the right thing?

Chapter 6

Cassie closed her eyes. The blues song playing through Ryan's car stereo system matched her mood.

Tension radiated from Ryan as he drove in silence back to the northern beaches from the city.

She pressed her lips together, unsure of what to do next. The few times she'd tried to initiate a conversation, he'd given her curt, single-word responses.

He drove onto her street and pulled up outside her apartment complex. The streetlights illuminated the hard line of his mouth.

She attempted a smile. "Thanks for taking me to the dinner."

He nodded. "Have you changed your mind?"

"About?"

"Sean." He gripped the steering wheel with both hands.

Her stomach tensed. "What about Sean?"

"Will you contact him?"

"I'll probably call him sometime."

"Why?" He met her gaze head-on. "What do you hope to achieve?"

Yesterday she'd had no interest in seeing Sean again. How had tonight changed her perspective on him?

"I'm not lending him money, if that's what you're thinking," she said.

"What's the point?" He looked away. "Haven't you got better things to do than hang out with my loser brother?"

She recoiled, his harsh tone feeling like a slap in the face.

"I need closure," she said, squaring her shoulders.

"How will seeing him help you?"

"I'd like to hear his side of the story."

"You know the facts. Listening to him won't make a difference."

She frowned. "I'm not so sure."

"He's a user, and he only contacted us because he's desperate for money."

"Or maybe, in some bizarre way, it's his cry for help?"

He shook his head. "You don't get it. He's beyond help. A lost cause. The only thing he wants is free money."

"I don't believe anyone is beyond help." Anger pulsed through her. "Just thinking about Sean makes me mad."

He nodded. "Me, too."

"And it's going to be tough, but I know I need to work on letting go of my anger and hurt so I can move on."

"You're going to let him off the hook?"

She lowered her lashes, taking in a deep breath. "I'm far from perfect and we all make mistakes." She disengaged her seat belt.

"That's not the point."

"But it is." She bit her lower lip to stop it from trembling. "Do you think people should hold every bad thing you've ever done against you forever?"

Tonight she'd experienced the full force of her own human weakness. She'd been so close to falling off the wagon, and her self-control had been stretched to the limit.

"Sean's actions over the last few years can't be written off as little mistakes," he said.

"I know."

"He has screwed up big-time."

"But it's not my job to judge him—"

Ryan thumped his fist on the steering wheel. "You're wrong about Sean, and you're not helping him. How will he ever learn to be responsible?"

Tears pricked her eyes. Ryan's grudge against his brother ran deep.

Anger and frustration warred inside her. She understood Ryan's anger. A part of her wanted to give in and tell Ryan what he wanted to hear. Smooth over the stormy waters and make things good between them again.

Ryan stared straight ahead out the windshield. He tapped his fingers hard on the dashboard, stress exuding from every pore in his body.

Compassion for his situation filled her heart. His brother had betrayed him. The magnitude of Sean's selfishness stole her breath.

Torn between two brothers, she couldn't see a way to resolve this issue right now. She hated seeing Sean on a mission to self-destruct. At the same time she longed to comfort Ryan, but she couldn't tell him what he wanted to hear.

A no-win situation. They all needed time to process the events that had transpired tonight.

Minutes later she broke the silence. "I think I should go inside."

"I'll walk you to your door." He jumped out of the SUV, slamming his door before striding to her side of the vehicle and opening her door.

"Thanks." She walked next to him up the drive.

He quickened his pace, not glancing at all in her direction.

She fell behind, unwilling to risk twisting her ankle or ruining her heels on the uneven pavement by attempting to keep up with his cracking pace.

She approached the entrance to her apartment building, scrounging around in her purse for her keys. She fumbled with the lock.

"Here, let me." He took the keys out of her hand.

She looked up at his face, catching a glimpse of the pain in his eyes before he shuttered his expression.

He unlocked the door, holding it open for her.

"Thanks." She crossed the threshold into the foyer.

He placed her keys in her hand. "See you later."

Dismissed, she stood in the foyer, watching him race up the drive to his SUV.

He gunned the engine and sped away.

She trudged up the two flights of stairs to her apartment, her despair growing with each step. This wasn't how their evening was supposed to end.

She closed her apartment door, kicked off her heels and strode into the living room.

Julia glanced up from the armchair across the room. "Hey, I didn't expect you back for ages." She pressed the stop button on the remote control.

Cassie sprawled out on the sofa. "I'm so glad you're home."

"I got back early." Julia frowned. "What's wrong?"

"You won't believe what happened tonight."

"I'm sorry. I know you wanted things to work out with Ryan—"

"This isn't just about Ryan, although everything with him is a mess, too."

"Oh." Julia ate a spoonful of vanilla ice cream. "Did your dad do something?"

"No, but I also managed to upset him big-time. Sean turned up."

Julia's eyes widened. "You're joking!"

"I wish I was."

"What happened?" Julia placed her ice cream bowl on the coffee table and sat next to her.

Cassie told Julia about Sean's reappearance and her disagreement with Ryan.

"I'm so sorry." Julia passed over a box of tissues. "Did you know about Ryan repaying the money to your father?"

She shook her head. "It explains why Dad didn't pursue criminal charges with the police."

"And why Ryan is furious with Sean."

Cassie mopped up the tears at the corners of her eyes. "Then our stilted goodbye outside turned into another argument. I think it's all over between us before it ever really started."

"Did Ryan tell you he never wanted to see you again?"

"No, but he didn't suggest we go out again."

Julia frowned. "Does Ryan want to forgive Sean?"

"Yes and no. Sean needs to prove to Ryan that he deserves to be forgiven before Ryan will consider forgiving him."

"I'll make us some hot chocolate" Julia gave her a big hug. "Hopefully Ryan will calm down in a few days."

"I don't think this is going to blow over. I've had a bad night, and I nearly had a drink."

"What? Oh, Cassie, you poor thing. Was this after Sean turned up?"

She nodded, gnawing her lower lip. "I walked to the bar and came so close to having a drink. I thought I'd recovered enough that I wouldn't be easily tempted but…"

"You've had a stressful night."

"I know."

Concern filled Julia's eyes. "I also get why you'd feel the urge to blot it all out."

"I feel terrible. I've been sober for so long, and one moment of weakness almost undid everything."

"But you didn't have a drink. Did you pray?"

She nodded. "It helped, and reminded me of the early days of my recovery when it was a full-on daily battle to stay sober."

"Cass, it's hard, but you stood firm and didn't give in."

"But I came close to caving and telling Ryan what he wanted to hear, and now I've lost him."

"Does it bother Ryan that you and Sean were once close friends?"

"I don't know." She sighed. "He didn't like the idea of me hanging out with Sean. Not that I intend to do that."

Julia stood. "I'll get the hot chocolate."

"Thanks for listening."

"No problem."

Cassie slouched on the sofa, her heart heavy. How could an evening that started so well end in such a horrible mess?

Why did Sean have to reappear tonight, of all nights? Now she had the added problem of her father being annoyed with her.

She couldn't shake the feeling of doom over her relationship with Ryan.

Cassie slipped into a spare seat beside Julia toward the back of Beachside Community Church. She glanced around the building, hoping to find Ryan among the evening congregation.

A week had passed since the disastrous dinner, and Ryan hadn't contacted her. Each morning she searched the crowd waiting for the ferry, hoping to catch a glimpse of him. Even Laura hadn't seen him.

Maybe he'd been interstate with work? She'd considered asking her father before remembering she wasn't his favorite person at the moment. Earlier in the week Laura had listened to her father rant about her rude behavior at the dinner. Could anything else go wrong?

She stood for the opening song. The familiar words about God's grace and love washed over her, bringing her a small measure of comfort.

After everything that had happened with Ryan, she'd never actually found out why he'd been challenged by Simon's sermon a few weeks ago. She still didn't know for sure if he was a believer.

She missed Ryan. None of the single men she knew through church set her heart racing or captured her thoughts like he did.

She blinked away the moisture building in her eyes. It was time to stop moping and get on with her life. Shedding more tears wouldn't change the situation.

Julia elbowed her in the side and leaned toward her. "Guess who just slipped into a row, two in front of us on the far right?"

Cassie followed Julia's gaze. She raised her hand to smother a shriek.

Ryan stood still, his attention focused on the overhead screen at the front.

What did this mean? Would he talk to her after the service or rush out the door after the closing song?

Before long Simon stood to deliver his sermon. Cassie listened with rapt attention, refusing to glance in Ryan's direction.

By the time she stood for the closing song, she could no longer hold back and did her best to catch Ryan's eye.

He glanced in her direction, nodding in acknowledgment before returning his attention to the words on the screen.

The song ended and he waved.

Julia smiled. "It looks like he's heading your way. I'll make myself scarce."

"I don't know what to expect and I don't feel like arguing with him again."

"Stop stressing. Most people don't go to church looking for a fight." Julia turned away and started talking to someone in the row behind.

Cassie spun around to find Ryan standing two feet away from her.

He looked tired, as if he'd been working too hard or hadn't been sleeping well. His eyes lacked their usual spark.

She smiled and waited for him to break the awkward silence between them.

"How's your week been?" he asked.

"Busy. And yours?"

"Hectic. I've done three interstate trips this week."

She nodded. Maybe she'd been too quick to judge him over his lack of communication this past week.

"Have you seen Sean yet?" he asked.

"No."

He paused. "I thought you were keen to see him and become friends again."

Friends? Did he think she wanted to hang out with Sean? "I've put off phoning Sean because seeing him again will be difficult. His appearance last weekend was a big shock for me, too."

Ryan raked his hand through his hair. "But you still intend seeing him."

Cassie nodded. "Have you seen or spoken to him?"

His eyes hardened and a frown marred his handsome face. "No, and I can't say I'm unhappy about that, either."

"What did your parents say about Sean's brief reappearance?"

"I haven't told them."

She lifted a brow. "Why not?"

"What can I say to them? It will hurt them to hear about Sean's behavior at the hotel."

"But wouldn't they like to know that you've seen him in person?"

"It's not that easy." He crossed his arms over his chest. "How would you like to tell your parents that you've seen your long-lost brother, but he's still as selfish and unrepentant as before?"

The angry tone in his voice stunned her into silence. What could she say that wouldn't inflame the situation further?

The uncomfortable silence continued and Cassie nibbled her lower lip. She understood Ryan's pain and hurt over Sean, but avoiding him wasn't necessarily the best solution.

Ryan met her gaze. "Life is unfair. My parents are good people and they don't deserve a son who treats them as badly as Sean does."

"But Sean has problems and he needs help. Your parents could try and help him—"

"My parents have suffered enough." He rubbed his hands over his weary face. "I'll tell them about Sean in person when I visit them in a few weeks. Mom's too heartbroken to hear this news over the phone."

"Ryan, I'm sorry. I realize this is difficult—"

"Do you? Do you understand the full extent of the pain and suffering that Sean has inflicted on us? If you did, you wouldn't be so quick to try and forgive and forget."

"Wait a minute." She placed her hands on her hips. "Who said it would be quick or easy? Did you hear what Simon said tonight about forgiveness?"

"Yeah, and I have issues with his ideas on forgiveness."

"What bothers you?"

"The Bible talks about God being just and fair. I can't see any fairness in this forgiveness stuff you've all been talking about."

Cassie sucked in a deep breath. "Why don't you talk to Simon? I'm sure he'd be happy to discuss his sermon."

"You know, I think I will."

She held his stormy gaze. "Would you like to join me for coffee?"

He shook his head. "I've got an early flight tomorrow so I must run. I'll look into meeting with Simon later this week."

"Sure."

"See you later." He strode toward the exit.

She let out a big sigh. It could have been much worse. There had been no raised voices during their conversation, and he'd kept a firm grip on his rising anger. Would he lose control if he saw Sean again?

She focused on the good news from their conversation. Ryan wanted to talk to Simon. His conversation with Simon might not go well, but he was prepared to talk about his issues. A good starting point.

This coming week she'd work up the courage to call Sean and arrange a meeting. She'd prefer to avoid him, but the time had come for her to address the issues in her past. She couldn't put off seeing Sean any longer.

Chapter 7

The following Saturday morning Cassie strolled along The Corso, passing the numerous restaurants and cafés lining the promenade as she headed toward Manly Beach. She glanced up at the clock in the middle of the pedestrian thoroughfare.

Her stomach tightened. Five minutes to go. Would Sean bother turning up?

During her tense phone conversation with Sean last night, he'd insisted on brunch at a beachside café they used to frequent. She hadn't set foot in that café since he'd left.

She approached the ocean promenade, and the aroma of ground coffee mixed with the salty sea breeze brought a smile to her lips. The familiar blackboard sign stood outside the café. Doubts plagued her mind. Had she made the right decision?

Cassie stared at the soothing ocean. The rhythmic pattern of the rolling waves calmed her pulse. She stepped inside the café, inhaling a deep breath.

Sean sat at their usual corner table with panoramic ocean views. Sporting a suntan and wearing a casual T-shirt, he fitted in with the local clientele. His intense blue gaze scoured over her.

She flinched, resisting the urge to run.

He indicated the seat beside him and she chose to sit opposite, her back facing the view.

He raised an eyebrow. "You don't want to look at the ocean?"

"I'm fine here."

"Your loss." He drained his coffee mug.

How long had he been waiting? Had he arrived early to secure his favorite table?

She attempted a smile. "You've ordered?"

"Only coffee." His eyes softened. "Are you hungry?"

"Yes, but I'm not sure what I feel like."

"I'm ordering the big breakfast with the works."

Did he intend footing the bill for his breakfast or expect her to pay for his decadence? Cynical thoughts kept crowding her mind.

She nibbled her lower lip. How could she give him a fair hearing if she kept judging him by her previous experiences?

She perused the menu. "I'll have eggs Benedict."

"I didn't know you liked your eggs that way."

"Things change. People change."

A waiter arrived and wrote down their order.

Sean stretched out in his seat. "It's like old times."

"Not really."

"Come on, you remember our weekend ritual of brunch right here at this table."

She straightened her back, wriggling in her seat. "If it was so good, why did you take off?"

"It's complicated."

She twisted her hands together in her lap. "Tell me about it."

"Not much to tell."

"I'd like to hear your side of the story."

He frowned. "What did your dad and Ryan say?"

"Enough. I know why you took off in a hurry."

"Then you've got to understand I didn't want to be hauled off to jail."

She looked him straight in the eye. "Why did you take the money? Dad paid you a decent salary."

"It wasn't enough."

"That's ridiculous. You were paid top dollar compared to similar jobs elsewhere."

"I did it for you. I was going to surprise you with a diamond solitaire engagement ring during our trip to Vegas."

She gasped. "We were drunk when you talked about Vegas. That trip was never going to happen."

"But you must have known how I felt about you."

She shook her head. "We were friends, that's all."

He smiled. "I know you had feelings for me."

She ignored his comment, recognizing it was a distraction. "I want to know why you took the money."

"I needed to clear some debts and leave your dad's company."

"I can't believe you thought you'd get away with it."

"I nearly did. If only that idiot contractor hadn't queried his invoice on my day off."

She lifted a brow. "You must have known you'd get caught."

"And you never did anything bad and never got caught? I can think of a few examples...."

Dark memories threatened to bubble to the surface. "Stop changing the subject. Stealing fifty thousand dollars is a big deal."

"I don't get why you're being so self-righteous. What do you think paid for your drinks and our nights out?"

"No way! You're not shifting the blame to me."

He leaned forward in his seat. "But I did this for you, for us."

"There is no us. If I'd known the truth, I wouldn't have accepted the drinks."

"Really? Are you sure about that?"

Shame filled her heart. *Lord, please forgive me. I'm thankful I'm a different person now.*

A waiter returned with their meals and she ate her breakfast, unable to forget the past.

She sipped her latte. "Why didn't you tell me the truth? I could have helped you."

He laughed. "Who are you kidding? You would have run to daddy with a sob story to save yourself from being implicated."

"Dad deserved to hear the truth. After all, you were stealing from him."

"You would have abandoned me and been glad when you heard I went to jail. It was always all about you."

Her jaw dropped. His words stung like a cold glass of water thrown on her face. The mirror from the past sitting opposite her didn't present a pleasant picture.

He cut a bacon strip into bite-size pieces. "Don't look so stunned. That's why we got on so well. We're two of a kind."

She sighed. "I'm sorry."

"I heard you got religion. Guess that means you now live a boring life."

"What? I live a fulfilling life—"

"Spare me the details. I went to Sunday school and it didn't do me much good."

She took her time chewing her food. Too many revelations had unsettled her.

"How's my brother doing?" he asked.

"Fine."

"He still mad at me?"

She frowned. "Ask him yourself. You know his number."

"Aha. I knew it. Did he dump you after I showed up?"

She ate another mouthful and remained silent.

"It's not too late for us," he said. "You'll get past this religious phase and—"

"No!"

"Isn't that why you contacted me?"

She shook her head. He couldn't be more mistaken about

her motives for this meeting. "I want to know when you'll start clearing your debt to Ryan."

"This is getting old. Ryan's loaded and he won't miss a few thousand dollars."

"Sean, you need to repay him. It's the right thing to do."

"Whatever." He finished eating his breakfast.

"I want to help you, but you've got to look at things from Ryan's perspective. If you repay the money, you can start working toward rebuilding your relationship with him."

"Why would I want to do that?"

"Ryan's your brother—he's family."

"Don't lecture me on families. I hear you're still not getting on with your father."

"I'm working on it." She'd made plans to have dinner with Dad next week.

"Why don't we go out tonight?"

"I don't drink."

He stared at her. "You're serious?"

She nodded. "My sobriety's very important."

He pushed back his chair and stood. "I'm outta here. Tell Ryan I'll contact him when I need something."

"What?"

"He took it upon himself to fix my last big money problem. Next time I'll call on him myself." He tossed two twenty-dollar notes on the table and sauntered out of the café.

She placed her head in her hands. He wasn't prepared to listen to reason. What more could she do?

A few years ago she'd been like a boat without an anchor, blowing in whatever direction the wind took her. Now her faith provided her with a stable foundation, and she prayed Sean would find his anchor soon before it was too late.

Cassie pressed the doorbell at her father's home. The musical chime irritated her and raised her anxiety another notch.

She peeked at her watch. Eight-thirty. Right on time for the late dinner she'd organized with Dad.

The door opened and her father smiled. "Come in. I've ordered Indian."

"Butter chicken?"

He nodded. "Plus korma and the curry you like. You'll have leftovers to take home."

"Thanks, Dad." Her mouth watered over the prospect of Indian cuisine. Dad had ordered her favorites, an excellent sign. Indian food was his usual peace offering. He'd accepted her apology for rushing off with Ryan at the dinner.

She followed him through to the dining room. Piles of documents were spread out over one half of the ten-seat mahogany table.

"You look busy," she said.

"I'd hoped to have all this finalized before you arrived."

"That's okay." She understood his work was important. He'd keep on working through dinner, scanning documents and half listening to her.

He continued to sort papers into various files. "Would you like a cool drink?"

"I'll make a jug of iced tea. And you?"

"I'm still going on my coffee."

"At this time of night?"

"I'll be up past midnight and catch a few hours of sleep before waking at dawn."

She frowned. "I worry about your health. Do you have time to exercise and eat three proper meals a day?"

"I'm fine." He waved away her concerns. "I have more important things to think about."

Like work. His life revolved around work. Why couldn't he see past his obsession with work and realize there was more to life?

"Has Laura found a wedding dress?" he asked.

She shook her head. "We're going shopping again in a few weeks."

"Why doesn't she get that designer in Double Bay to put something together?"

"She still hasn't decided on the style and color."

"At least I've got one daughter who can make a fast decision."

She smiled. "Thanks, Dad."

He raised an eyebrow. "For what?"

"For saying something nice."

"I always say nice things about you."

She sucked in a deep breath. *Let it go.* So far the evening was working out much better than she'd anticipated.

"I'll go make the tea," she said.

He nodded. "Dinner should arrive soon."

She returned with her iced tea. Her father remained seated, glasses on as he scanned through documents.

He looked up. "How's work going?"

"Fine." She pressed her lips together. He never changed. As usual, he inquired about work first. Why couldn't she accept this was his way?

"Are you up for a promotion?"

She shook her head.

"You should apply for something else."

"I have." There, she'd said it. For better or worse.

He raised an eyebrow. "Internal or external?"

"Queensland. A sister company to my current hotel chain."

He sat back in his chair and met her gaze. "When did you apply?"

"Weeks ago and yesterday I learned the date and flight details for my interview at the island resort."

He smiled. "Good luck. I'm sure you'll do well, and it's about time you focused on furthering your career."

What did he think she'd been doing for the past few years? The doorbell chimed. "I'll get it."

She opened the front door and widened her eyes. "Ryan."

* * *

Ryan nodded. "Hi, Cassie."

Confusion clouded her face. "You don't have Indian food?"

"Huh?" What was Cassie doing here? He'd recognized her car out front.

She looked past him to the road. "The home delivery person should arrive soon."

"I've got documents for your father."

She took a step back. "Come in."

A beaten-up hatchback pulled into the drive, and Ryan paused in the doorway. "Looks like your dinner is here."

"Excellent." Her eyes lit up. "I'm starved."

His stomach sank. Food held more appeal for her than his presence. Not a comforting thought. "I'll carry it in for you."

"Thanks." Her mouth almost curved into a smile.

He collected the food and followed her through to the dining room. She strode ahead in silence, her back straight and unyielding.

John sat at one end of the table, absorbed in reading some papers. He glanced at Ryan. "Thanks for finalizing that deal for me."

"No worries." He hovered at the entrance of the room. "Everything's in order."

Cassie turned to her father. "I'll fetch the plates and cutlery."

"Set the table for three. Ryan, have you eaten?"

He shook his head. "I'll grab something on the way home."

"Please stay and join us," John said.

"I don't want to intrude."

Cassie gave him a polite smile. "We've got plenty of food."

Ryan frowned. She didn't want him to stay, but John

needed to check the documents. Work came first. "Sounds good."

"I'll be back in a minute." Cassie walked toward the kitchen.

He couldn't blame her for being annoyed. At church a few weeks ago he'd spoken out of anger before leaving in a rush. Later at home he'd gone a few rounds with his punching bag. Even then, his fury over Sean's behavior hadn't diminished.

Cassie deposited a tray with glasses and a jug of iced tea on the far end of the table. She left the room without glancing once in his direction.

Ryan shook his head. How could he improve their relationship tonight? What would it take to convince her that she was wrong about Sean?

He handed an envelope of documents to John. "Everything's here that you'll need. Tomorrow I'll email the supporting documentation to London."

"Great. Thanks for rushing this through at the last minute."

"No problem." He dropped into a chair and loosened his tie. The rest of the week shouldn't be too hectic because his other projects were on track.

Cassie returned with plates and cutlery. Sapphire earrings hung from her lobes and her navy suit added to her air of cool professionalism.

"Here, let me help," Ryan said.

"Thanks." She passed the cutlery, her fingers skimming over his hand.

He paused, meeting her startled gaze. Her mouth parted, and he remembered the sweet kiss they'd shared on his yacht. He wanted a repeat performance.

Why did Sean have to return and mess everything up? Things had been going so well between him and Cassie before Sean ruined it.

She sat opposite Ryan. "Dad, can I please say grace?"

John shrugged. "If you insist."

She closed her eyes, appearing to ignore her father's gibe. "Lord, thanks for this delicious dinner and good company. Amen."

Ryan glanced over at John. A cynical expression covered the older man's face.

She opened her eyes. "Please, Ryan, help yourself."

"Thanks." He served up his food and tasted a sample. The aromatic spices tingled in his mouth. "This is good."

"These guys do the best Indian food in Sydney." She took a mouthful, her eyes sparkling.

If only he could stare into her mesmerizing eyes all night and put aside his issues with Sean.

He ate some butter chicken. "Wow, this melts in your mouth."

"It's her all-time favorite," John said. "I'd be in trouble if I ordered Indian and forgot the butter chicken."

"But I can't eat it too often," she said. "Too many calories."

John's phone rang. He glanced at the screen and accepted the call, listening for a minute before turning to Cassie. "I'm sorry. I need to take this call and I might be a while."

"Don't let your dinner go cold," she said.

"I'll take it with me." John picked up his plate and left the room.

Ryan cleaned up his first serving of butter chicken. "I guess it's just the two of us."

"I'm yet to have dinner here without an interruption."

"At least you're not eating alone." He added a second serving of butter chicken and basmati rice to his plate. He'd try the korma next.

"True." A wistful expression flitted across her face. She reminded him of a little girl who missed her daddy.

"Have you seen Sean?" he asked.

"Yes." She lowered her lashes.

Anger stirred inside him. "How did it go?"

"Not well."

He nodded. His brother would never change, and Ryan hoped she'd now listen to him. He'd told her this would be the inevitable outcome.

"Are you seeing him again?"

"I don't know." She played with the food on her plate. "Ryan, he needs help. His life is spiraling out of control."

He stabbed a piece of chicken with his fork. "Not my problem."

"How can you say that? He's your brother."

"Why are you on his side?"

"This isn't about sides. I had a revelation after my conversation with Sean."

"Which was?" This had better be good. He refused to listen to more excuses for Sean's bad behavior.

"I could still be walking in the wilderness like Sean. Lost and without any direction in my life."

He frowned. "But you're not. Sean's an adult, not a small child. He needs to grow up and take responsibility for his choices."

"I know."

He widened his eyes, her words sinking in. "You agree that enabling Sean to continue along his current life path isn't helping him."

"Yes, but Sean doesn't see things from this perspective."

"Did he ask you for money?"

She shook her head. "He threatened to harass you for more money because you fixed his last money problem."

"He'd better not." Sean wouldn't see one more cent from him until he repaid his debt.

She spooned some korma on her plate. "Why did you bail him out last time?"

Good question. At the time he thought he'd be helping his brother. Criminal charges were pending, his parents were distraught and Sean was missing. It had seemed like the right thing to do.

"I made an error in judgment," he said.

"Which made everything worse?"

He nodded. "My parents weren't coping well with Sean's disappearance, let alone the missing money."

"So you thought by repaying my father you'd alleviate some of their stress?"

"I was wrong." He raked his hand through his hair. "My decision hasn't helped him. He needs to apologize and make amends with everyone."

"I can't see that happening anytime soon."

Neither could he. Pain wrenched his heart. His brother had set his path and he couldn't save him this time. "Has he shown you any remorse?"

Hurt flickered in her eyes. "If anything he's happy he got away with it."

How typical of Sean. "Do you still intend to forgive him?"

"I don't know what I want to do."

He held her gaze. "I know this is hard."

"I want to help him fix his life."

"I'm not sure that's possible."

She nodded. "His heart is hard and he's in a really bad place."

Last week Ryan had met with Cassie's pastor. The subject of forgiveness had come up during their conversation. He still had more questions than answers, and Simon wanted to talk further about Ryan's opinion on forgiveness.

He tightened his grip on his glass. "Why do you care so much about my brother?"

She sighed. "I feel partly responsible."

"How can that be possible?"

"I encouraged him to party and introduced him to people who were a bad influence."

"It's not your fault. You didn't force him to make bad decisions."

"But I failed him back then and I want to make things right now."

He reached for her hand. "It's not your job to rescue him."

She nibbled her lower lip. "But I'm not going to turn my back on him, either."

He nodded. "I'm sorry I took my frustration with Sean out on you." He drew in a deep breath. "Can we get past this?"

She squeezed his hand, her gaze soft. "Yes. I want to get to know you better."

Her words warmed his heart. "Are you busy tomorrow night?"

She smiled. "Dinner together two nights in a row?"

"Why not?" He couldn't think of anyone he'd rather have dinner with tomorrow night.

Chapter 8

A few weeks later, Laura stood in front of a full-length mirror. "This dress is the one."

Cassie smiled. "Are you sure?"

Laura twirled around in the spacious fitting room. "With a V-neckline and a different pattern for the beading and sequins, this dress would be perfect."

"You like the straight skirt?" Her sister had tried on dozens of wedding dresses today, and the majority had a full skirt of some description.

"This ivory silk fabric is just divine. The line of the dress is stylish and the train is buttoned on so I can remove it at the reception. This is the one."

"Excellent." Cassie slumped into a plush seat in the corner. Her feet ached from spending her Saturday traipsing all over Sydney searching for the right dress for Laura. Mission accomplished.

Her sister preened in front of the mirrors, inspecting the dress from all angles. "Calista can alter the neckline. Do you think the skirt will sit right?"

Cassie grinned. "You look beautiful. I can't see anything wrong with the line of the skirt, and Calista has measured you to ensure it's a flawless fit. Stop fretting."

"I'm so excited. My wedding day is getting closer. Less than a hundred days to go."

"Why don't you get changed and I'll let Calista know

you've made a decision." Exhaustion washed over her. She needed a coffee.

"Okay, I'll need your help unbuttoning the back."

Cassie unfastened all the tiny pearl buttons down the back of the gown. She left Laura in the fitting room and found Calista deep in conversation with another customer.

Calista's assistant approached her. "How's Laura doing?"

"She's made her decision and is getting dressed."

"That's great news. Would you like a coffee while you wait?"

She nodded. "Thanks." There had to be advantages to shopping at an exclusive bridal boutique in Double Bay.

"I'll bring a tray out shortly."

She sank back into the leather sofa, glancing around the boutique. Wedding dresses worth tens of thousands of dollars surrounded her.

Calista finished with her customer and caught Cassie's eye. "You should try the cream silk on."

She widened her eyes. "Why?" Her gaze returned to the cream silk strapless gown.

"It would look fabulous on you," Calista said. "You have the right body shape to pull it off."

Laura emerged from the fitting room and admired the wedding dress Calista held on a hanger. "I'm all done. You've got yourself a sale so I won't need to try anything else on."

"That's wonderful, darling. I'd love to see Cassie try this one on."

Laura beamed. "So would I." She turned to Cassie. "All day you've watched me try on dresses. Now it's your turn."

"But I'm not getting married."

"One day a smart man will snap you up," Calista said. "I saw the photo of you and Ryan Mitchell in the society pages. You two make a great couple."

"Ryan's a great guy, but I don't need a wedding dress."

"Come on, Cassie, indulge me. When I designed that gown, I'd envisaged someone like you wearing it. Remember, not all my brides are as beautiful as you two."

Laura giggled. "I'll take a photo with my phone, if that's okay."

Calista nodded.

"All right, I give in. I'll only do a quick on and off fitting. No fancy stuff."

"Promise," Laura said.

Cassie followed her sister into the fitting room. "I'm going to need your help with all these buttons," she said.

Laura's smile widened. "My pleasure."

She changed out of her clothes and stepped into the bridal gown. Laura helped her pull up the dress and fasten the buttons.

She spun around in front of the mirrors.

"Wow," Laura said. "You look sensational."

The gown was beautiful and she looked like a bride. "If I ever need a wedding dress, I know where to come."

She gathered up the skirt of the gown and walked to the front of the boutique.

Calista smiled. "Stunning. This dress was made for you, darling."

Tears welled behind Cassie's eyes. Would she ever be a bride? A vivid picture of Ryan formed in her mind. He'd make a handsome groom, cutting a dashing figure in a suit.

"Okay, show over." She lowered her lashes, holding back a few tears. "Laura, please help me with the gown."

Calista snapped a photo. "I'll note the details for you. I've a hunch you'll be back before long."

Calista's assistant returned with a tray of coffee. The sweet aroma distracted Cassie and urged her into action.

She'd enjoy her coffee while Laura finalized the details of her bridal gown purchase. Would great coffee help her forget her daydream about being Ryan's bride?

* * *

Later in the afternoon, Cassie followed Laura into the elevator leading to Greg's apartment.

"Please stay for dinner," Laura said. "It's the least I can do to thank you for all your help."

"I don't want to interrupt your plans with Greg."

Laura waved away her concerns. "I suspect Greg's slouched on the sofa watching football."

"Please don't make me watch football."

"I won't. The wedding invitation samples are upstairs. We can't make a decision and I'd appreciate your input."

The elevator beeped and Cassie stepped inside with her sister. The doors closed and they began the upward ascent to Greg's floor.

Laura examined her fingernails. "Did I mention Ryan might be watching football with Greg?"

"No, did it slip your mind?"

"Cassie, don't be like that. Oh, I've chipped my nail again."

"You'll cope." She suppressed a smile. Ryan had sent her a message a few hours ago, letting her know he was at Greg's apartment for dinner. Laura's matchmaking would go into overdrive if she knew about the message.

"You two are meant to be together." Laura's eyes twinkled. "I'll show Ryan the photo of you trying on the bridal gown. That should inspire him to take action."

"No!" She tightened her grip on her purse. "Okay, here's the thing. We are finally getting past the whole mess with Sean and moving to a better place, and we don't need your matchmaking help."

The elevator door slid open and Laura smiled. "You can't blame me for wanting to see you marry Ryan."

She ignored Laura's comment and followed her inside Greg's apartment.

Her heartbeat quickened. Ryan sat beside Greg on the sofa in the living room.

"Hi, guys," Laura said. "We're celebrating tonight. I found my dress."

Greg stood and gave his fiancée a hug. "That's great news."

"And I've invited Cassie to dinner. Ryan, would you like to stay?"

Ryan's warm gaze swept over Cassie. "Greg's already lined me up to man the outdoor grill after the game finishes."

Cassie nodded, holding his warm gaze for a few moments.

"Excellent," Laura said. "We'll see you after the game."

Laura turned away and Ryan winked.

Cassie stifled a giggle and followed Laura out of the room.

After spending an hour with Laura selecting wedding invitations, Cassie carried the coleslaw to Greg's dining table and laid out the cutlery for four places. The aroma of grilling meat wafted in from the balcony.

Ryan stood outside in her direct line of vision. Arms crossed, he leaned back against a pole near the balcony railing. The gusty breeze blew smoke from the grill around the spacious balcony. Sunglasses shaded his eyes, but she could feel his gaze upon her.

Cassie smiled, her pulse racing. She looked forward to spending some time alone with Ryan after dinner, if they could escape Laura's schemes.

She arranged the place settings and admired the stunning views of Manly Wharf and Sydney Harbour through the eighth-floor panoramic windows. Hues of pink and orange lit up the sky over the western horizon. She finished setting the table and returned to the kitchen.

Laura sat on a stool at the kitchen island.

"Is there anything else you need me to do?" Cassie asked.

Laura shook her head. "I'm all done. If you could take

the bread to the table, I'll round up the boys. The meat should be ready by now."

She followed behind Laura, balancing a platter of French bread and selecting a seat overlooking the windows. Laura sat opposite and Greg pulled out a chair next to his fiancée.

Ryan came inside, holding a tray of sizzling meat. He slipped into the spare seat beside her.

"Laura, can we please say grace?" Cassie asked.

Laura sighed. "I guess so."

"I'd be happy to say grace for us," Ryan said.

Cassie's jaw fell slack. Had Ryan been talking to Simon?

Greg shot Ryan a questioning glance. "Since when do you say grace before you eat?"

"We grew up offering a blessing before all our meals. An old habit I should resurrect."

Greg shrugged. "Be my guest."

Cassie closed her eyes and pressed her lips together. Laura and Greg didn't understand her faith. She couldn't expect them to be enthusiastic about Ryan's desire to explore his faith and she prayed their lack of interest wouldn't deter Ryan.

"Dear Lord," Ryan said. "Thanks for this food and good friends. Amen."

"Amen." Cassie opened her eyes and turned to Ryan. "I appreciate you saying grace for us."

His smile broadened. "You're welcome."

She selected a steak and served up a generous portion of salad and bread. A large glass of chilled water completed her meal.

Ryan and Greg piled their plates high with meat.

Laura laughed. "It's a good thing Cassie and I aren't big meat eaters."

"We're celebrating, too," Greg said.

Ryan grinned. "Adventurer won the handicap race for her yacht class."

"Congratulations," Laura said. "Here I was thinking you two had been watching sports all day on television."

Cassie smiled. "How are you tracking in the overall scores?"

"We're in the top three," Ryan said.

"What happens when you miss a week to go up to the Blue Mountains with us?" Laura asked.

Ryan shrugged. "I'll sort something out. No big deal."

"It's next weekend." Greg said.

Laura nodded. "Cassie, were you able to rearrange your work schedule?"

"Yes, my leave is approved."

"Excellent," Laura said. "I can't wait to go hiking and mountain biking."

Ryan's smile widened. "Sounds fun."

"By the way, I saw Sean in Manly a few days ago," Laura said.

Cassie lifted a brow. "Why didn't you mention this earlier?"

"I didn't want to cause trouble. He said hello but then took off. I got the impression he didn't want to talk to me."

"Typical," Ryan said. "He's too gutless to face up to the consequences of his actions."

Cassie groaned. "Hopefully he'll get to the point where he realizes he needs help."

"Don't count on it," Ryan said.

Laura frowned. "I think Cassie is right. He's on a downward spiral and he'll get to the stage where he needs you to help him."

"Maybe, but he's not getting any more money out of me," Ryan said.

"I agree," Laura said. "Money isn't going to help him. You all know Sean isn't my favorite person. But Ryan, he's your brother and if he's in trouble you should be there for him."

Ryan stabbed his fork into a piece of steak. "How can

I support him in a constructive way if he doesn't want my help?"

"Have you called him on his cell phone?" Cassie asked.

"Waste of time. My parents have left dozens of messages and he won't return their calls."

Greg frowned. "If Sean doesn't want to be found, then there's not much Ryan can do."

"He contacted me," Cassie said. "Maybe if you left a message he'd contact you, too?"

"He doesn't owe you money," Ryan said.

"True, but I promise you, when Sean's ready to accept help I'll be there if you need me."

"Thanks," Ryan said. "I hope he turns his life around, but I'm a realist. It doesn't look like it's going to happen anytime soon."

Cassie finished her last mouthful of steak. She remembered all the help her mother, Laura and Julia had provided when she made the decision to quit drinking. She suspected Sean's road to recovery would be difficult.

Laura rose from the table. "Greg, can you please help me in the kitchen while I organize dessert?"

"I'll help," Cassie said.

"No, Greg and I will fix everything. You and Ryan can relax and talk."

Laura and Greg cleared the table and retreated to the kitchen.

Ryan smiled. "I think Laura wants us to talk."

"She's not subtle and she mentioned Sean for a reason."

"You didn't tell her that I messaged you?"

"She doesn't need to know everything that happens in my life."

He grinned. "I'm looking forward to next weekend."

"Me, too." She was staying in the downstairs one-bedroom apartment with Laura. Ryan, Greg and the newlyweds, Anna and Craig, would be upstairs in the main part of the house.

Ryan's eyes shone with hope and his thumb circled over her fingertips. "I've been meeting weekly with Simon to talk about stuff."

Wow. She hadn't expected to hear this good news. "Has he been helpful?"

"He's had some interesting things to say. We've been discussing forgiveness and my brother."

"Sean's situation is complicated. Eventually he might come to see your point of view, but he'll need to deal with some of his issues first before he'll work this out."

"Why do you think that?"

"I've been there." Memories of those dark days filled her mind. "It took time for me to understand that I'd hurt others and needed to make amends."

"What made the difference for you? What turned your life around?"

"My faith. I discovered God's unconditional love and realized I needed Jesus."

Ryan frowned. "Sean and I both grew up in the church. We attended Sunday school when we were kids, but I don't get this. It doesn't make sense."

"I'll be praying for you."

He nodded. "Would you like to go to the movies after dessert?"

"I'd like to see the new romantic comedy that's just been released."

He raised an eyebrow. "A chick flick?"

"Can you cope?"

"Next time it's my turn to choose."

"Sounds good." She looked forward to the first of many movie dates.

The following evening Ryan stood in the Beachside Community Church for the closing song. He mumbled the words as the congregation lifted their voices in song. The unfamiliar chorus about God's grace didn't make a lot of sense, but everyone else seemed to understand the message from the song.

The service concluded and Cassie turned to him. "Have you got time for supper?"

He shook his head. "I'll be up at dawn tomorrow to catch an early flight to Brisbane. Maybe another time?"

"Sure. What did you think of the sermon?"

"I can relate to the older brother. He did the right thing and worked hard. Why should his younger brother be welcomed back by their father with a big celebration?"

"That's the whole point of the parable of the prodigal son. The father loves both his sons and was happy when his wayward son returned to him."

"I think the older son was ripped off. Why should the younger son, who squandered his money, share in the spoils?"

Simon appeared beside him. "Ryan, I overheard your question and we can talk more over coffee this week."

He nodded. "I'll be in touch."

"No problem. Catch you both later." Simon turned away, greeting a man behind them.

Cassie smiled. "I'm glad you're talking to Simon. He's good at explaining things."

"Yes." Ryan wanted to discover the truth. Cassie and Simon had an inner peace and contentment that he desired. "What are you up to this week?"

"I've got a job interview in North Queensland on Tuesday."

He widened his eyes. "You're planning to leave Sydney?"

"I've been thinking about it for a while."

What? Disappointment shot through him. Why hadn't she mentioned this earlier? "Are you staying there overnight?"

She shook her head. "I'm flying out at six for a midmorning interview at the island resort before returning late in the afternoon."

His stomach sank. Why bother dating him if she intended to move away?

"Good luck." He dragged his mouth into a smile. "I hope the interview goes well."

A part of him also hoped there would be fierce competition for the position. He didn't want her to move away.

"Thanks. I'm a little nervous as I haven't done a formal face-to-face panel interview in ages."

"I'm sure you'll be fine." What about her aspirations to help Sean? How could she help his brother if she moved to Queensland?

"I wanted to stay overnight, but I have to work on Wednesday."

He wouldn't mind indulging in a day trip to North Queensland with Cassie. He'd still be in Brisbane on Tuesday morning. Maybe he could reschedule his appointments for that day? "You may be living there on a permanent basis soon."

Her eyes lit up. "I'm excited about the prospect."

He nodded, unable to share her excitement. Long-distance relationships didn't work. His move to London had brought an abrupt and painful end to a two-year relationship with a previous girlfriend. He wasn't prepared to travel down that road again.

His life was in Sydney, and he didn't want to move away. There was no work for management consultants on a tropical island.

Doubts filled his mind. His enthusiasm over the prospect of building a relationship with Cassie had dimmed. He'd enjoy the journey while it lasted, but a future between them seemed uncertain.

Cassie threw her keys in a dish on the hall table in her apartment and headed into the kitchen. She found Julia making two mugs of hot chocolate.

Julia added marshmallows to their mugs. "Have you spoken with your father again about the Queensland job?"

Cassie shook her head. "He's due back from London soon, and I'm still surprised by how supportive he is."

Julia raised an eyebrow. "I thought he might have some concerns."

"About what?"

"Okay, please don't take this the wrong way. Have you thought about the implications of living on an island resort with easy access to liquor?"

"I'll be fine. I work in a hotel now and it isn't a problem."

"But these holiday resorts are different. They've got indoor bars and outdoor bars by all the pools. There are bars everywhere. I care about you and can't help being concerned you'll fall into temptation."

"Honestly, I don't think it'll be a problem."

"Really?"

"I'm stronger now."

Julia frowned. "You think so."

She nodded. "I know so."

"What about the charity dinner? You didn't feel so strong then."

"That's different. Sean had just reappeared and I was under extreme stress."

Julia sipped her hot chocolate. "Okay, it's your decision. But remember, you won't have your family and friends close by to support you."

Cassie followed Julia into the living room and sat beside her on the sofa. "Ryan's not happy, either."

"You mentioned the job to him tonight?"

She nodded. "I should have said something on Saturday at Laura's, but she's upset about the whole idea so I kept quiet."

"What about at the movies last night or this afternoon before church?"

Her heart constricted. "I didn't want to spoil our time together."

"Did he say much?"

She shook her head. "I could tell he's disappointed. His work is in Sydney. I don't know—maybe it's a bad idea."

"Your travel plans for the interview are all set. Do the interview and see what happens. You may hate the place."

"I doubt it. I've dreamed about doing this for a long time, but I'm not interested in a long-distance relationship."

"Take one step at a time, and wait until you're actually offered the job before you fret too much."

"You're right. I have to trust God to lead me in the right direction."

"It will all work out one way or another."

Cassie nodded. She hoped and prayed Julia was right.

Chapter 9

The next morning Cassie flicked through the documents in her in-tray. Ten event orders needed to be finalized this week, two by the close of business today.

She placed the two urgent ones on top of the pile. Both brides had made numerous changes to their wedding reception arrangements over the past few months, and she awaited their response to her emails and phone calls. Why did people leave everything to the last minute?

She grabbed her purse and coat before heading out of her cubicle.

She detoured via Colleen's desk. "I'll be back in forty-five minutes."

Colleen raised an eyebrow. "Are you meeting Mr. Gorgeous for lunch?"

"No such luck. He's in Brisbane today and I'm catching a quick bite with my sister at The Deli House."

"Have fun. I'm swamped and no one's returning my calls. Can you please bring me back a salad on rye?"

"No problem. See you soon." She made her way to the bay of elevators and checked the clock on the wall. Five minutes past midday. Late again. Laura wouldn't be impressed.

Before long the elevator deposited her on the ground floor. She strode through the lobby, struggling into her coat.

Rain poured down over the busy street. She waved to Damien, the concierge, before exiting the hotel.

The wind blew the rain in sheets across the road. An umbrella would be useless. She stepped onto the marble pavement and a screech of brakes startled her.

She spun around and her ankle collapsed.

"No." Her body hit the ground, her thick coat buffering her fall.

Searing pain shot up from her ankle. *Not now.* Her interview was tomorrow and it had already been postponed once so she couldn't reschedule.

Damien raced over to her. "Are you okay?"

She pressed her lips together and nodded. Tears filled her eyes.

He pulled out his cell phone and spoke in low tones before ending the brief call.

"Colleen's on her way with a first-aid kit."

"Thanks." She removed her low-heeled shoe, cradling her ankle in her hands. The swelling showed through her flesh-toned stockings.

Damien frowned. "You were having a good run for a while there."

"I know. It's nearly a year since I last sprained this ankle."

The rain eased to a light sprinkle and the hotel awning gave her shelter. She swiped her damp hair back off her face.

"For what it's worth, you fell gracefully. Just like in the movies," Damien said.

Great. How embarrassing. Her cell phone rang and she rummaged through her purse, checking the caller ID. *Ryan.*

"Hi, Ryan."

"Cassie, are you okay? You don't sound too good."

Tears rolled down her face. "I've sprained my ankle."

"What?"

"I'm outside the hotel, in the rain, with my ankle ballooning."

"Is someone helping you?"

"Yes."

Damien hovered nearby, concern etching his face.

"What happened?" Ryan asked.

"I was rushing to meet Laura for lunch and slipped on the wet pavement."

"How bad is the sprain?"

"Pretty bad." She moved her leg into a more comfortable position. Her ankle protested and she stifled a moan. "It really hurts."

"I hope you haven't broken any bones."

"Me, too. My interview is tomorrow."

"I assume you can still do it. I'd hate for you to have to cancel."

She paused. "Why? I thought you weren't crazy about the idea."

"I'm not, but it's your dream, something you really want. Don't let a sprained ankle stop you."

She lifted a brow. He understood her need to chase her dream job. "The doctors might tell me to rest tomorrow."

"You could use a wheelchair at the airport."

"What?"

"Just a thought."

She considered his suggestion. "You're right. I might need a wheelchair."

"I know."

She groaned. *He thinks he has all the answers.* Piercing pain radiated from her ankle and she tightened her grip on the phone, sucking in a deep breath. "Thanks for being supportive."

"I'm worried about you. Has first aid arrived yet?"

Cassie glanced around and Colleen appeared at the hotel entrance. "Coming now."

"Good."

She looked over her shoulder. "I can see Laura, too."

"Say hi to her from me. I'd better go."

"Thanks for calling."

"I'll call you later today."

"Okay."

"Take care of yourself."

"Bye." She ended the call and shoved her phone in her purse.

Colleen arrived, crouching beside her. "I need to take you next door to the medical clinic."

Cassie nodded.

"Damien, can you please get us a wheelchair?" Colleen asked.

"Certainly." Damien disappeared inside the hotel.

Laura rushed to Cassie's side. "Are you okay?"

"I think we're having lunch at the medical clinic. Colleen, can my sister tag along?"

"Absolutely," Colleen said, turning to Laura. "You can duck out and get us lunch. I'm not sure how long we'll be waiting to see a doctor." She stood and stepped back a few paces.

"No problem." Laura looked down at Cassie. "I can't believe you've sprained your ankle again."

She nodded. "The wet pavement was slippery. It's not my fault."

Laura rolled her eyes and picked up Cassie's shoe. "The grip has worn on the sole. No wonder you slipped."

"Oh." She inspected the heel. "I'm buying a new pair this week." Not only were they comfortable, but they matched her favorite suit.

"From the look of your ankle you won't be wearing pumps for a while." Laura frowned. "I tried to call you a few minutes ago, but your phone was busy."

"Ryan called just after I fell."

Damien returned with a wheelchair and they all helped Cassie into the seat.

Colleen pushed the wheelchair and Laura walked beside her. Within minutes they were inside the medical clinic and Colleen excused herself to talk with the receptionist.

Laura pulled up a chair beside Cassie's wheelchair. "When's Ryan due back in Sydney?"

"Tomorrow afternoon."

"Are you canceling the interview?"

She shook her head. "I have to go."

"What about your ankle?"

"I'll use crutches, a wheelchair, whatever it takes to get me there."

Laura pursed her lips. "What did Ryan say?"

"He's very supportive."

"I don't get it." Laura narrowed her eyes. "I thought Ryan agreed with me. Don't you think this accident is a sign you shouldn't go?"

"I'm not canceling my interview."

"Your ankle might be broken and traveling might make it worse."

She sighed. "I know you don't want me to go."

"Can you blame me? I don't want you to move away."

"But a change of scene, hot weather all year round, will be good for me."

Laura pouted. "I'll miss you."

"I'll miss you, too." The hardest part would be leaving Mom and Laura.

"Then ditch the interview and stay in Sydney."

"I can't." Cassie met her sister's stormy gaze. "I have to go."

"Why?"

Cassie pressed her lips together. Pain gnawed at her nerves and fatigue overwhelmed her. Laura couldn't conceptualize her desire for freedom and independence from her family and old life.

"I want a new start." She hoped to rebuild her relationship with Dad before Laura's wedding and her potential move to Queensland.

"What about Ryan? You do realize leaving Sydney will destroy any chance you have of a future with him."

Her lower lip trembled. "I know."

"He's an ambitious man and moving to North Queensland will kill his career."

She nodded. "I'd never expect him to move."

Laura threw her hands in the air. "What are you thinking? Cancel the interview and find a new job in Sydney."

"What if things don't work out with Ryan? Then I've thrown away an excellent career opportunity for no good reason."

"Cassie, make things work out between the two of you." Laura took hold of her hand. "He cares about you. Do whatever it takes to fix your problems."

Whatever it takes? Cassie shook her head. Laura didn't get it. If only it was that simple.

The pain from her ankle pierced her heart. She wanted to please Ryan and make everything right, but she couldn't ignore her faith. Right now he was exploring his faith, but her niggling doubts remained. There was no guarantee that he'd end up making a commitment, and she couldn't marry a man who didn't share her faith.

Cassie rose to her feet, tucking her crutches under her armpits to take the weight off her sprained ankle. She shook hands with the five members of the interview panel.

Sara Scott, the human resources manager, stayed behind while the other panel members filed out of the room.

Cassie placed her injured foot on the ground, stifling a groan. "Thanks for the opportunity to interview for this position."

"Thank you for traveling all the way up here. We'll be in touch in about two weeks."

"No problem."

"I understand the difficulties you're having getting about so I've organized for Mike to drive you around and show you the facilities in one of our golf buggies."

"Sounds fun."

Sara handed her a visitor's sticker. "When's your charter boat due?"

She glanced at her watch. "In just under three hours."

"A buffet lunch is served in the Terrace Restaurant. I'll add you to the visitors list."

"Thanks, I appreciate all your help."

"I have another interview due to start in fifteen minutes, otherwise I'd show you the facilities myself. Have a great day and a safe trip back to Sydney."

Cassie slipped on her backpack and hobbled out of the meeting room. The brilliant blue of the ocean, visible through the large floor-to-ceiling windows, brought a smile to her lips. Imagine working with a spectacular view every day.

The plush carpet muted the sound of her hopping along the hallway. The elevator opened and she descended to the ground floor.

She approached the brunette behind the front desk. "Hi, I'm looking for Mike."

The brunette waved at someone behind her and a fair-haired young man wandered over.

"I'm Mike," he said, pointing to the front entrance. "Please follow me."

She emerged from the lobby to find a white golf buggy waiting at the door. Mike helped her shift her crutches and backpack behind their seats. She slipped into the seat beside him and he switched on the engine.

"The road system is basically one big circuit," Mike said. "I'll do a quick run around for you. I assume you want to stay seated to rest your ankle."

She nodded. "Thanks. I'd appreciate it."

"You're welcome. I heard you're the front-runner for the job."

"Really? My interview only finished ten minutes ago."

"I overheard the panel interviewers talking in the lobby.

I'm right in guessing you're the only candidate using crutches today."

"There must be more candidates to be interviewed."

He nodded. "A couple, but I overheard them saying the last few have much less experience than you."

"Thanks for the insider info."

"No worries, we're like a big family here. Most employees live on the mainland, except for the big bosses and some of the night staff. We all get on well and hang out together. Life here is one big party, and I think you'll like it."

She beamed. A relaxed lifestyle in the sun. What more could a girl want?

They drove past the eighteen-hole golf course. Tennis courts and an outdoor pool were situated next to the health club.

Mike began his commentary. "The private villas are up ahead. Ninety percent of our guests stay in the main complex. There's a covered walkway between the health club and the main complex, and you'll see signs marking the roads up to the secluded villas."

She drank in the exotic vegetation and white sandy beaches. An island paradise.

He smiled. "Up ahead, around the bend, is our wedding chapel on the beach. The function room is located beside the chapel. They both seat two hundred guests and we have an eighteen-month waiting list for weekend bookings."

The old-fashioned chapel sat among the palm trees, and the function room opened out onto a deck above the beach.

"This area is self-contained and the dock is just around the corner. It's only a ten-minute walk from here to the main complex."

Wow. The beauty of the island exceeded her expectations. She'd love to get married here, too. No wonder they had a long waiting list.

"Did Sara mention you'd have an office at the back of the function center as well as in the main complex?"

She nodded, her mouth curving into a wide smile. She could live on the mainland and enjoy a half-hour boat trip to work each day. The perks included a complimentary room in the complex when she worked evenings, and free buffet meals were available in the Terrace Restaurant during work hours.

The reality of the job struck her. She could soon be living and working in a tropical paradise.

Lord, thank You for giving me this opportunity. I'd love to secure this job and live here, but what about Ryan? I'd have to choose between Ryan and the job. Please give me wisdom and help me to make the right decision if I'm offered this job.

Before long the main complex came into view.

"Where are you headed next?" he asked.

"The Terrace Restaurant."

"No worries. I'll drop you off at the main entrance. The Terrace is located on the first floor, overlooking the beach."

"Thanks, you've been very informative."

"You're welcome." He smiled and within minutes brought the vehicle to a halt. "I hope to see you again soon."

"Me, too." She stood on one foot and angled her body out of the buggy.

He passed over her bag and crutches. The crutches dug into her arms as she made her way into the lobby.

She paused by the entrance to catch her breath. Perspiration covered her brow. The humidity outside had taken its toll and her hair had blown loose during the buggy ride. Next stop would be the ladies' room to freshen up.

She pushed wisps of hair back off her face and gripped the handles on her crutches. *Time to get moving.* She glanced up and noticed a tall man striding toward her.

Her pulse raced as she recognized his walk. Her gaze met his. *Ryan.* What was he doing here?

Chapter 10

Cassie dropped her crutches and collapsed into Ryan's arms.

"Hey," Ryan said. "You've been overdoing it."

She inhaled his earthy scent. "Probably."

He swung her backpack over his shoulder, hooked his arm under her legs and carried her toward the lounge area.

"Thanks." She relaxed in his embrace. The rhythmic pattern of his heart beating through his lightweight casual shirt brought a smile to her lips.

He lowered her onto a cushioned sofa.

She lifted a brow. "What are you doing here?"

"Taking you to lunch." He retrieved her crutches from the floor and sat beside her.

"What about work?"

His gray eyes sparkled. "I rearranged my schedule, and I'm flying back to Sydney with you this afternoon."

"Wow, I'm stunned. It's great to see you."

"When you've caught your breath, I'll escort you to the seafood restaurant upstairs. I've been assured the lobster is to die for."

"Sounds fantastic. I appreciate your help in getting around."

"Is your ankle really sore?"

She nodded. "I'm due for more painkillers soon."

"Are the crutches hurting, too?"

"Yep. I'm still getting the hang of them."

He grinned. "I can carry you to the restaurant."

"No way. I can do it. Everyone will think we're honeymooners."

He swept a wisp of hair off her face. "Is that such a bad thing?"

"But it's not true." *Yet.* His fingertips lingered over her forehead and images of the wedding chapel warmed her cheeks.

"Are you sure you're feeling up to it? I could get a wheelchair?"

"I'm fine." She inhaled a steadying breath. "But I might need one later."

"I thought so." He held her hand. "I'm here to take care of you."

Oh boy, she loved the way he looked after her.

Cassie hopped beside Ryan to the elevator, and they made their way to the second floor.

The exclusive restaurant overlooked the ocean on two sides, and she drank in the breathtaking views. This could be her new place of work, but what about Ryan? It wouldn't be the same without him here by her side.

The maître d' escorted them to a table positioned near the windows and a waiter appeared with leather-bound menus. No prices were listed, and a delectable selection of seafood dishes whetted her appetite.

Her mouth watered as they made their choices.

The waiter disappeared and Ryan reached for her hand. "So, tell me about the interview."

She placed her hand in his. "It went well. I'm happy with the answers I gave and I think I have a good chance of securing the job."

He sipped his iced water. "Is this what you really want?"

"I love the location. Look around us. Tropical paradise, fresh air, sunshine—what more could I want?"

"You've done a tour of the island."

She nodded. "It's gorgeous. The wedding chapel and

function center are beautiful and it's no surprise they have a long waiting list."

"Sounds great."

"If only my ankle wasn't injured and we had more time to explore the island. Mike told me there's a lot to see, and the island has eight beaches plus an inland lake."

"Mike?"

"He works here, and he gave me a quick tour in a golf buggy. He also mentioned that I'm the front-runner for the job."

He raised an eyebrow. "How would he know?"

"He overhead members of the interview panel talking about me. Anyway, he said the staff all hang out together and have lots of fun."

"I'm sure they do. But did you really take a close look?"

"What do you mean? There are holidaymakers everywhere, looking relaxed and enjoying the tropical surroundings."

He cleared his throat. "What about all the bars? By the pool, at the health club. Everywhere you turn there seems to be a bar of some description."

She shrugged. "No big deal. I work in a hotel and it comes with the territory."

"You think so?" He paused. "Aren't you at all concerned about the temptation to drink?"

"I'm fine. It's no different from Sydney."

He shook his head. "Do Mike and his work friends party hard?"

"I guess so." She let go of his hand, sitting taller in her chair. "But that doesn't mean I'm going to do the same thing."

"But what if all your new friends here love to party? Will it be so easy to avoid temptation?"

"I've been sober for nearly two years."

"That hasn't stopped you from being tempted."

She narrowed her eyes. "What are you talking about?"

"The charity dinner." He held her gaze, his tone firm. "I watched you stop by the bar and salivate over the bottles on display."

"Oh." She lowered her lashes, shame filling her. "Not my finest moment."

"Cassie, I'm proud of what you've achieved." He raked his hand through his hair. "But I'm worried you're unnecessarily putting yourself in the way of temptation if you choose to take this job."

She pursed her lips. "So it's not that you'll miss me. It's all about the likelihood of me falling off the wagon."

"Of course I'll miss you. I'm concerned because I care about you."

"But this is my dream job. For years I've wanted to leave the city and move to a place exactly like this."

"Did you conceptualize this dream at a time when you were living a party lifestyle? I imagine this job would be very appealing if your goal is to party."

His words hit her hard and her doubts resurfaced. She wanted to leave behind her old life in Sydney, but would this job create a whole new set of problems?

"I'll think about it, but I'm not convinced this job would be bad for me."

Their waiter arrived with a prawn appetizer.

He nodded. "It's your decision to make."

The job or Ryan. How could she choose? Her dream job versus her dream man.

Ryan rubbed his hands over his eyes. John's brisk voice sounded through the speakerphone on Ryan's desk. The lights in the neighboring buildings illuminated the night sky outside his office window.

"That's my update from London," John said. "Anything else I need to know about?"

"No. The Brisbane trip went well and I should be out of

here soon." *Hopefully before midnight.* He glanced at the time on his computer screen. Eleven thirty-six.

"How's Cassie doing?"

He frowned. "She had her job interview today, and we had lunch at the resort before flying back late this afternoon."

"Aha. That's why you're working so late."

"I caught up on work this evening, and I'm on schedule to leave for Melbourne tomorrow afternoon."

"How did her interview go?"

"Too well." He tightened his grip on his pen. "She's confident she's got a good chance of being offered the job."

"Is she aware of your thoughts?"

"Yes. We had a difference of opinion over the wisdom of her working in a party environment." Ryan had dropped the subject after their tense conversation over lunch, but his concerns remained.

"I hope you didn't tell her to turn down the job."

"Why?" What was John not telling him?

"She's stubborn, and I learned the hard way to say nothing. If I gave my opinion, Cassie always did the exact opposite to prove me wrong."

That explained a lot. Would Cassie do the same thing to him, as well? He twirled the pen between his fingers. She seemed more mature than John gave her credit for. "What do you think of this job she's chasing?"

"I'm happy she's seeking to advance her career." John paused. "But I agree with you. It's the wrong environment and I'm worried she'll start drinking again."

"What do you suggest I do?" He valued John's opinion.

"Back off and don't push the issue."

"That's going to be hard. All she talked about this afternoon was this wretched job."

"If you push her, she'll dig her heels in. Hopefully she'll work out for herself that it's the wrong move to make."

"Yeah, I can see your point. It's the same with me and

Sean. He always does the opposite of what I tell him he should do."

"Have you heard from Sean?"

"Not yet." Renewed anger began to build within him. "I called him again today and left a message. I told him if he doesn't contact me by next week, I'm going to hire someone to track him down."

"Good plan. Sean had better stay away from Cassie. If he hurts her again…"

If Sean did anything to upset Cassie, he'd have to answer to Ryan. He refused to tolerate his brother's inappropriate behavior. "You do remember Cassie's the one who arranged their last meeting."

John huffed. "Foolish girl. Has she seen him again?"

"No, and I don't think she's trying to contact him, either."

"That's a relief. I need you to take care of Cassie and keep Sean away from her. I don't trust him."

"That makes two of us. She'll be with me this weekend. It's Greg and Laura's weekend away for their bridal party."

"That's good news. I trust you to take care of my girl. Look, I must go. My next appointment is here."

"No worries. I'll be in touch tomorrow."

Ryan ended the call and stifled a yawn. Silence penetrated his office. Everyone else had left hours ago. He'd pack up soon and catch a few hours of sleep at home before returning to the office early tomorrow morning.

His work never ended, but today it had been worth it. He'd shared a fun day with Cassie.

She wanted a fun job. Did a fun job that paid well exist? Work and fun were mutually exclusive concepts in his world.

Simon enjoyed his job, and he had challenged Ryan to consider what would happen if he died tomorrow. Would his financial success and career achievements mean anything? Were relationships more important to him than money?

His immediate answer had been that relationships were definitely more important. But Simon had gone one step further and reminded him that his priorities in life were demonstrated by how he spent his time.

Sure, he'd taken the day off today, but it was nearly midnight and he was still at the office catching up on work. He could list a stack of reasons for why he was here, and with John overseas he couldn't delegate much of his workload.

Work ruled his life. He even put off sailing if he needed to work. He canceled visiting his folks if work commitments cropped up. Was it worth it?

Cassie's decision to move forward with her job application hit a raw nerve. In the past he'd ditched relationships to chase a new and better career opportunity. Now the boot was on the other foot, and he didn't like it one bit. How could she consider choosing her career over a relationship with him? He hated the idea of being her second choice.

This weekend he'd work on changing her mind. Prove to her that a future with him was far superior to an island resort job. Today had been a good start.

Sean had better contact him soon. John would go berserk if Sean harassed Cassie. Not that Ryan could blame John. His own protective instincts were on full alert, and he'd do whatever it took to keep Cassie safe from harm.

Late Thursday afternoon Cassie hobbled into her mother's kitchen and opened the fridge. The painkillers hadn't kicked in to dull the ache from her ankle.

The interior door to the garage slammed shut and she heard her mother bustle through the house.

Her mom appeared at the entrance to the kitchen.

"Hi, Mom. How was work?"

"Busy as usual. Have you been resting that foot and following your doctor's instructions?"

She nodded. "I've been good today, and the cab ride home from work helped." For the past few days she'd been staying with her mother to avoid the two flights of stairs in her apartment building.

"Sit down and I'll fetch whatever you need," Susan said.

"I'm hungry."

"I'll bring you some fresh fruit before I start making dinner."

Cassie hopped over to the counter and collapsed on a bar stool. "These painkillers aren't working."

"Your trip to Queensland on Tuesday was too much. You should have stayed here and rested."

"But I really want this job and I'm glad I went."

Susan's frown deepened. "Has Ryan phoned about the weekend?"

"I sent him a message a few hours ago. He's probably still on his way back from Melbourne."

Her mother switched on the coffeemaker. "I don't think it's a good idea for you to go away this weekend."

She sighed. "Laura would never forgive me if I backed out."

"What are you going to do up there? Stay at the house while everyone else is enjoying the outdoors?"

"It will work out okay, and with any luck I won't need these horrible crutches to get around."

The doorbell pealed and Susan glanced at the clock on the wall. "I've no idea who that could be." She walked out of the kitchen.

"Cassie, you have a visitor," her mother called out.

She wriggled around on her stool and smiled.

Ryan stood three feet away, holding two dozen yellow roses.

"They're beautiful, Ryan. You shouldn't have gone to so much trouble."

"I wanted to surprise you." He handed her the roses and placed a gentle kiss on her lips. "How are you feeling?"

Her pulse quickened and her usual optimism returned. "Okay." Much better now that she'd seen him.

"Good. I have something else to cheer you up." He gave her a wrapped gift box.

She opened the present and laughed. "You're a lifesaver. This is just what I feel like."

"Between flowers and chocolate I couldn't go wrong."

She inhaled the distinctive fragrance of the roses. "They're gorgeous, and such a vivid yellow."

"The florist guaranteed they'd cheer you up." He gazed into her eyes. "Would you like me to make coffee?"

She nodded. "I feel so useless at the moment."

"You'll be walking again soon."

"I hope so."

He poured the coffee and passed a steaming mug to her. "Have you coped okay at work?"

"Sort of. I mostly stay at my desk because my ankle's still really sore." She added milk and sugar to her coffee. "But I have the next three days off."

"Are you still coming up the mountains with us tomorrow night?"

She nodded. "Mom doesn't think I should, but I don't want to disappoint Laura."

"Do you want to go?"

She sipped her coffee. "I do, but I don't want to spend the whole time at the house while you guys are out having fun."

"I have an idea for Saturday."

"Such as?"

He grinned. "It's my surprise, but I promise you'll like it."

"Please tell me."

"No way. You can wait two days until Saturday."

"Two surprises in one week. Come on, spill it."

He shook his head.

"Are you ticklish?" She edged her bar stool closer to him.

He laughed. "You're out of luck."

"Not fair."

"I'll be around to collect you about this time tomorrow."

Her cell phone rang. She glanced at the screen. Private number. She connected the call. "Hello."

"Hi, Cassie."

"Sean? Where are you?"

"I can't talk long. I need to see you this weekend."

"I'm out of town."

"Where?"

"Katoomba, with Laura and Greg's bridal party."

"Good. I'd rather meet you away from Sydney."

"Why?"

"It's complicated. What's the address?"

"Tell me what's wrong."

"I can't. It's not safe."

She gasped. "Are you in trouble? Is someone after you?"

"I'll tell you in person. What's the address?"

"Smith Street. I can't remember the number but it's the house at the end with views called Rose something."

"Okay. I've got to go."

"Sean, wait."

The phone disconnected.

Cassie groaned and turned to Ryan. "As you heard, that was Sean."

"Is he in trouble?"

She nodded.

"What does he want?"

"He wants to see me this weekend."

He frowned. "Did he say why?"

She shook her head. "I think someone's after him."

"Debt collectors. That's nothing new."

"I got the impression he's concerned for his safety. He's happy I'm out of town this weekend, and it's like he'd prefer to meet me away from Sydney. Something's very wrong."

Ryan nodded. "He has probably borrowed money from

one of those loan sharks and they're after him to recoup their cash."

"Do you think they'd hurt him?"

"Who knows? He may have crossed the wrong person this time. I was afraid that would happen."

"I'm really scared for him. He sounded agitated."

"Did he call from his phone?"

She checked her caller list. "Private number. There was lots of traffic noise in the background so he probably rang from a pay phone."

"I'm not leaving you alone this weekend."

"Why? I can handle Sean."

"Can you handle the nasty people who may be following him?"

She gasped. "You think he might put me in danger?"

"It sounds like he's trying to keep a low profile for a reason. Why else would he travel all the way to Katoomba to talk to you?"

"I don't know. Maybe he realizes he needs help?"

"Or maybe he's going to hit you up for a loan to repay the people he's hiding from. My parents and I have been leaving messages on his cell phone for weeks. Why has he contacted you again and not us?"

She widened her eyes. "Do you think he knows you'll be there, too?"

"The bridal party details were listed online under the photos from Laura and Greg's engagement party. I'm guessing that's how Sean knew we'd be together at the charity dinner."

"I'm not lending him money."

"I agree. He may be contacting you to get to me."

She shuddered. "He's going to make good on his threat."

"It's not going to happen." A grim expression shadowed Ryan's face. "I'm going to sort out this mess once and for all."

Chapter 11

On Saturday morning Cassie gazed out the window of Ryan's SUV at the brown undulating hills, covered in patches of grazing sheep. They'd stayed at the holiday house in Katoomba last night and headed out straight after breakfast, traveling farther inland on the Great Western Highway.

Ryan pointed to a clump of trees on the horizon. "The homestead is on the rise behind the trees."

"Is this your big surprise?" Why did he think she'd be interested in visiting a farm?

He smiled. "I grew up on this farm."

Her mouth gaped open. Ryan had once lived here? "Do your parents still own it?"

"My friends live there. My parents sold the farm to Lisa's dad and then, a few years later, she married Tim, one of my old friends."

"Interesting."

His smile broadened. "Yeah, and before Dad sold the farm everyone had expected me to marry Lisa."

She lifted a brow. "How old were you?"

"Twenty. I was studying in Sydney and too ambitious to settle for life on the farm."

"Lisa didn't consider moving to the city?"

He turned left onto a gravel road. "She's a country girl. We've kept in touch over the years."

She nodded. He understood her need to pursue her

dream job, although he'd voiced his concerns about her sobriety and highlighted glitches in her plan.

The SUV bumped along an unsealed dirt track and the homestead came into view. Ryan parked under a shady gum tree near the house.

Native plants grew along the edge of the drive and a wide veranda surrounded the brick home. A tall brunette holding a small child waved from the veranda.

"Lisa and Tim are looking forward to meeting you," he said.

"Okay." He'd told his friends about her?

He walked up the front path beside her. She shoved her sunglasses on her head and snuck a glance at Ryan. His taupe polo shirt and khaki cargo pants accentuated his muscular physique.

Twinges of discomfort radiated from her ankle, slowing her pace. At least today she could hobble short distances without the crutches.

Lisa gave Ryan a hug before turning to Cassie. "I'm glad I finally have a chance to meet you." She smiled. "Come inside and rest your ankle."

Lisa's friendly greeting put her at ease and she flopped on a comfortable sofa in the living room, smoothing her long skirt over her knees.

A dark-haired boy, who looked no older than four, threw himself into Ryan's arms.

"Hey, little man, good to see you." Ryan said.

Lisa's smile widened. "Brett's our exuberant youngest child."

Brett settled on Ryan's knee and Ryan gave the boy his full attention, whispering in his ear.

The little boy grinned and laughed.

Cassie's heart melted. He'd make a great dad. She couldn't remember receiving her father's undivided attention, except for the times when she'd upset him. Dad had yelled at her for hours after Sean disappeared with the company money.

"Daddy went fishing on the boat." Brett jumped off Ryan's knee, landing on his bottom on the carpeted floor.

"Your daddy's a lucky man," Ryan said.

Lisa laughed. "He still talks about all the boats he spotted from Ryan's apartment."

"Daddy catches big fish." Brett stood and raced outside, banging the screen door behind him.

"Tim went fishing with Ben, our eldest, first thing this morning and should be back soon."

"What are the girls up to?" he asked.

"Linda's upstairs buried in a book and Katie's outside riding her bike."

"I'd like to show Cassie around the property. Should we go now or after lunch?"

"Do you mind if we have a late lunch?" Lisa glanced at her watch. "Tim promised me they'd be back by now."

He grinned. "They probably lost track of the time. We'll go now and return within an hour."

"Tim's motorbikes are in the shed or you can take the tractor. Would you like a drink or a snack before you go?"

Cassie shook her head. "I'm good. We stopped for coffee in Bathurst on the way." She held Ryan's hand and rose from the sofa, walking with him to the back door.

She frowned. "Aren't you forgetting something?"

Ryan opened the screen door. "Huh?"

"My ankle will make it difficult to ride a tractor let alone a motorbike."

"I figured you could ride with me."

"Is that a good idea?"

He nodded and led her along a paved path toward the shed. "I've had a bike license for years."

"Okay." She nibbled her lower lip. "You've noticed I'm wearing a skirt."

A slow smile spread over his face. "I've noticed."

"I don't want to ruin it with grease." *Or mud. Or manure. Ick!* "Why didn't you suggest I change into jeans this morning?"

"You look great in your pretty skirt, and it's easier for you to wear a skirt with your ankle all bandaged up."

Heat warmed her cheeks. "All right. I'll give it a go."

"You'll be fine. Tuck your skirt around your legs after you climb on the bike." He stopped in front of a large dirt bike and let go of her hand.

Cassie placed her hands on his broad shoulders to maintain her balance and settled on the bike behind him. She tucked in her skirt and circled her arms around his waist. "I'm ready."

The engine roared to life and Ryan guided the powerful bike toward the back of the farm. Flocks of sheep grazed on the dusty brown paddocks and congregated along the riverbank.

Cassie inhaled the fresh country air and a hint of Ryan's expensive aftershave. Sunglasses protected her eyes from the cool wind and a strong sense of freedom pervaded her mind. She started to understand Ryan's attachment to this land.

They drew to a halt near a large gum tree. A furry wombat ambled past, retreating to an underground burrow.

She jumped off the bike and pushed her tangled hair back off her face, her gaze roaming over the river and valley below. "It must look amazing when everything's green."

He smiled. "I love it here. The river is twice this size after the rains."

"Did you swim in the river?"

"All the time, and we had to watch out for snakes."

She shivered. "I wish you hadn't mentioned that. I don't want to see a snake today."

He stepped closer, cupping her cheek in his hand. "I'll keep you safe."

She held his warm gaze, her pulse rate accelerating. "I trust you."

His eyes softened and he lowered his head. She closed her eyes and his lips teased hers, inspiring her to deepen the kiss.

He wrapped his strong arms around her. She sighed and ran her fingers through his lustrous hair.

Ryan pulled back, his breathing shallow. "We should head back to the house."

Wow. Her lips tingled and she longed for a repeat performance. "Do we have to?"

"It's nearly time for lunch." He drew her back into his arms, holding her close.

Cassie rested her head against his chest, content to listen to his heartbeat. She didn't want this wonderful day to end.

Ryan changed gears on the motorbike and they flew along the dirt track leading to the homestead. Cassie leaned into his back, her arms wrapped around his waist. He smiled, memories of their kiss by the river lingering in his mind.

Tim waved in greeting as they drew to a halt near the shed.

Ryan helped Cassie off the bike and introduced her to his friend.

Tim shook Cassie's hand. "Good to meet you."

"I've enjoyed cruising around your property," she said.

Tim grinned. "Ryan likes riding my bikes."

"One of the perks of visiting here. Were the fish biting?"

"Yep. Ben nearly tipped the boat a few times trying to pull in his catch."

"Barbecued fish for lunch?" Ryan asked.

Tim nodded. "Lisa made her special marinade. I'd better go check on the grill."

Cassie smiled. "Can I help with anything?"

"No. Head on over to the back veranda and lunch will be ready soon." Tim strode ahead to the house.

Ryan followed behind with Cassie, his hand resting on her waist.

A large wooden table stood in the center of the long veranda. Lisa appeared with salads and bread, and the older children set out the plates and cutlery.

"Did you two have a fun ride?" Lisa asked.

Cassie nodded and dropped into the seat beside him. "Your property is huge."

"It keeps Tim busy," Lisa said.

The aroma of barbecued fish filled the veranda and Tim placed a large platter on the table. Ryan selected a few fillets and a generous serving of salad.

"Dad, can we go down to the river for a swim?" Katie asked.

"It's hot enough today," Linda said.

"Maybe later," Tim said.

Katie pouted. "You spent all morning with Ben and you promised yesterday you'd take us."

"Okay, sweetheart, but we have visitors today."

"They can come, too, can't they, Mom?" Linda asked.

Lisa sighed. "I need to stay here until Brett wakes up. Ryan and Cassie, what would you like to do?"

Ryan savored his first taste of the grilled fish fillet. "I'll help you clean up after lunch before we hit the road."

Cassie nodded. "I probably should rest my foot."

"Okay, that's settled," Tim said. "The children can be excused from the table when they're finished."

"Thanks, Dad," Katie and Linda said in unison.

Minutes later the girls cleared their plates and raced inside, Ben not far behind them.

Ryan grinned. "The girls are becoming a handful."

Lisa nibbled on a slice of home-baked bread. "One day they'll be old enough to do more things unsupervised. They're both petrified of snakes."

"I don't blame them," Cassie said.

"I'm surprised you didn't see any during your ride," Tim said.

"Cassie, do you remember hearing that swishing noise in the grass when we stopped off?"

She gasped. "It wasn't…"

"I saw a brown tail slink away toward the trees—"

"And you didn't tell me. It could have bitten us and I can't even run away."

He laughed. "You're so much fun to tease."

She playfully punched his forearm. "You'll keep. I'll get you back for that one later."

"Ryan, you shouldn't tempt fate," Lisa said. "Remember that time we all went to Blackrock Dam."

"And you and Sean couldn't run up that hill fast enough," Tim said. "Lucky your old man was nearby to save the day."

"I was only nine and that king brown snake was huge."

Tim shrugged. "Cassie, now you know he wasn't always so big and brave."

"Now wait a minute," he said. "Cassie doesn't want to hear any more boring old stories about our childhood."

"Have you heard from Sean?" Tim asked.

Ryan narrowed his eyes. "He's around, although he hasn't contacted Mom and Dad."

Lisa frowned. "I'm sorry. Your parents must be worried sick about him."

"I'm going to see my brother again sooner rather than later."

"How?" Tim asked. "If you're not in contact with him…"

Cassie rearranged the salad greens on her plate. "He's been in touch with me and I'm half expecting to see him this weekend."

Ryan speared a cherry tomato with his fork. "And I'll be there with Cassie to find out what's going on."

* * *

A few hours later Cassie stretched out her legs, stifling a yawn.

Ryan steered the SUV onto a gravel road. "Take a nap."

"Okay. I'm feeling tired, probably from the painkillers."

"No worries. We'll be driving for a couple more hours."

She closed her eyes, the warm sun lulling her to sleep.

They stopped moving and she sat upright. "Where are we?"

He unhooked his seat belt and opened his door. "There's a truck halfway in a ditch up ahead."

The back of a small truck angled precariously on the shoulder of the road.

She gasped. "I hope no one is hurt."

"Stay here and I'll check it out." He strode toward the truck and disappeared from view.

Minutes passed and her impatience grew. Did he need help?

She hopped out of the SUV and limped over to the truck. "Hey, what's happening?"

Ryan wriggled out from under the front of the truck, covered in dirt. "What are you doing? You need to rest that foot."

A gray-haired man appeared beside Ryan.

"Are you okay?" she asked.

The man nodded. "A roo jumped out of nowhere and I ended up here. I'm Bert, an old neighbor of Ryan's."

"Cassie." She shook Bert's outstretched hand. "Did you hit the kangaroo?"

"No, but I need to be towed out of here."

"Don't worry, Bert," Ryan said. "The underside looks intact and I've got ropes with me."

Bert slapped Ryan on the back. "Your dad would be proud."

Ryan headed back to his SUV and returned with the necessary equipment.

Cassie swiped a blowfly off her arm. The two men seemed to know what they were doing. "Is the truck drivable?"

"I hope so," Ryan said.

Bert chuckled. "Young Ryan here knows his way around machinery."

"Bert taught me a few tricks. Now we're ready to haul her out."

Cassie slid into the passenger seat and looked over her shoulder.

Ryan got in and shifted the SUV into gear. "Hold on."

They lurched forward and a cloud of dust engulfed the rear window.

He braked, leaving the motor running while he checked out the truck's progress.

A wide grin covered his face as he leaped back in his seat.

"Good news, I hope," she said.

He nodded, cutting the engine. "I'll grab some tools and help Bert give the truck a thorough check."

"Will you be long?"

"I hope not."

Before long he returned, frowning. "The truck appears to be fine, but we need to follow Bert back to his place just to be sure."

"Does he live nearby?"

Ryan cleaned his greasy hands on an old rag. "About thirty minutes in the opposite direction to where we're heading."

"Sure. It's more important for Bert to get home safely than to be on time. Laura can cope if we're late. But we should call or text so she doesn't worry."

"We should be in cell phone range soon."

Bert crawled along ahead of them and the drive to his home took longer than Cassie had anticipated. After declining Bert's invitation to stay for coffee, they backtracked to the main highway.

An hour later Cassie picked up a signal on her cell phone. She sent a message to Laura, explaining their delay.

Minutes later she read Laura's response. "Laura wants us to go straight to the restaurant, and she's bringing a change of clothes for both of us."

He glanced at his grease-stained polo shirt. "Did you tell her I'm covered in grease?"

She shook her head. "The eucalyptus oil has cleaned the grease off your hands. Didn't you say you had a spare sweater in the back of the SUV?"

He nodded. "An old one I use on the boat. Not exactly fine dining clothes."

"We'll be fine. A sweater will hide most of the grease and hopefully the restaurant isn't too posh." She looked forward to having dinner with Ryan tonight, the perfect end to a romantic day out.

The restaurant was located on the edge of a cliff. Darkness enveloped the valleys, hiding the magnificent views of the Blue Mountains.

Ryan draped his arm around Cassie's waist. They climbed the steps and entered the crowded room.

Laura waved from a table on the far side of the restaurant. He helped Cassie to her seat as the entrées were served.

Greg grinned. "I'm glad you guys could make it."

"We considered waiting to order, but the restaurant closes early," Laura said. "The chef is waiting on your entrée order and you'll have to skip the appetizers."

"That's fine," Ryan said. "We had a big lunch at the farm."

Laura eyed his clothes, wrinkling her nose. "Is that mud on you?"

"Plus a little bit of grease and dirt from the truck," he said.

"I'm glad I brought clean clothes for both of you."

"Thanks, Laura," Ryan said. "I'm looking forward to a hot shower later."

"We'll place our order, then change," Cassie said.

"A good idea," Laura said. "You know, Ryan, the weirdest thing happened earlier. Greg and I were outside in the front garden and we thought we saw Sean walking by on the other side of the road."

He raised an eyebrow. "What was he wearing?"

"Nothing distinctive. A very ordinary-looking pair of jeans and a gray sweater. A dark green baseball cap and sunglasses hid his face."

Cassie met his gaze, her eyes wide. "He wasn't bluffing when he called me."

Greg frowned. "What's Sean doing here?"

"We don't know." A steely tone entered Ryan's voice. "I'm sick of his games and I'm going to find out what's going on with him sooner rather than later."

Chapter 12

Later in the evening Cassie stared at the flames leaping around the fireplace in the holiday house.

Ryan handed her a mug of hot chocolate with marshmallows and sat with her on the leather sofa.

She snuggled back against a cushion, her legs stretched out in front of her. "That was a fast shower."

He ran his hand over his dark hair, still slick with water droplets. "I didn't want to miss out on spending time with you."

Silence filled the house, broken by the occasional cracking of the fire. The others had retired for the evening after they arrived back from the restaurant. A day of mountain bike riding had exhausted them, and tomorrow they wanted to do an early morning hike around Echo Point.

Ryan stifled a yawn.

She grinned. "Are you sure you're not going to fall asleep on me? I need your help negotiating the outdoor stairs to the apartment. I don't want to wake Laura by tumbling down the stairs."

"I'm wide awake and enjoying my time with you."

"You've had me to yourself nearly all day." She reached over and caught hold of his hand.

He dropped a gentle kiss on her forehead. "Not long enough."

Warmth flooded her heart. "Thanks for your surprise. Tim and Lisa are nice people."

"They'd like us to visit again."

She nodded, her gaze drawn to the flames in the fireplace, leaping and crackling around the wood. The unpredictable flames reminded her of Sean.

What did Sean want? Where was he staying?

Sean's words echoed through her mind. What trouble had he found for himself this time? Was he in danger? Could she and Ryan help him?

"You seem lost in thought," he said.

"I've been thinking about Sean."

His grip tightened on her hand. "Worrying won't help him. He'll turn up at an inconvenient time."

"Why do you say that?"

"He disrupted our date at the charity dinner. He'll turn up again and ruin something else."

"I think he's in more trouble than we realize."

He nodded. "But I'm not fixing his problems this time."

The resolute expression on Ryan's face convinced her he was serious. "Are you concerned for his safety?"

"Of course, he's my brother." Worry lines formed between his brows. "He always was unpredictable, even as a kid."

"Did you get on well with him when you were younger?"

"Most of the time, but he drove our parents crazy. He had a knack for finding trouble wherever he went, but he was fun to hang around."

She sipped her hot chocolate. "Do you think he's bluffing?"

"Who knows? These days he's not known for keeping his word."

"I can't help but worry. If he's in a tight spot we should try to help him."

He held her gaze. "Cassie, I know you have good intentions, but you can't fix Sean. Right now he doesn't want the right kind of help. Can we talk about something else?"

"Sure." She pressed her lips together, the logic of Ryan's

gentle reprimand sinking in. Julia had said the same thing to her last week. Her need to fix people often wasn't helpful for the other person. Or an emotionally healthy choice for her. If only Sean's predicament didn't tug at her heart....

Ryan twined his fingers through hers. "I'm glad your ankle gave us an excuse to spend the day together."

She stared into the warm depths of his eyes. "Me, too."

"I think we share something special." His thumb traced a line around her chin.

She nodded. She'd fallen in love with Ryan. The truth hit her hard.

Her stomach tensed. It was time to ask him the one question plaguing her mind.

"Ryan, um, I was wondering where you stand with God?"

His eyes widened. "Well, I've been praying and reading the Gospel of Mark."

She suppressed a squeal of pure joy, but she couldn't help but smile. *Thank you, Lord.*

"I've also been meeting with Simon, and some of his ideas are starting to make sense."

"That's great news."

"We've had a few long discussions on forgiveness."

"It can be hard to forgive people who have wronged us." Like her father and Sean.

He nodded. "Sean has wronged both of us."

"For me, it's not just about Sean." She drew in a deep breath. "I'm working on improving my relationship with my father."

"Things seemed good between you two at dinner a few weeks ago."

"Dinner went well and your presence helped."

"In what way?"

She stirred in the soft marshmallows, creating pink-and-white swirls in the chocolate milk. "We get on better when other people are around. It's during one-on-one conversation that things become heated."

"It's good your relationship with him is improving."

"Dad surprised me by being supportive about my job interview in Queensland."

"What if he hadn't been supportive?"

She lifted a brow. "What do you mean?"

"Hypothetically speaking, what if your father had said he didn't think it was a good idea for you to pursue the job. Would that change anything?"

She shrugged. "It's irrelevant because he told me he's happy I applied for the job."

"I value John's opinion. Would it make a difference to you if he had concerns about the job?"

"I guess I'd hear him out and try to understand why he holds a different opinion." This had proved to be difficult in the past when yelling had been their main form of communication. "But I make up my own mind and I pray first before making any decisions."

He nodded. "Sounds sensible."

Did Ryan feel awkward about her father being his boss? Dad spoke about Ryan in glowing terms. Ryan and Greg were like the sons he'd never had.

She suspected her father might even side with Ryan against her.

"What are you going to do if you're the successful applicant?" He tapped his fingers on the side of his mug. "Will you move to Queensland?"

She lowered her lashes. "I don't know. I guess it depends."

"On what?"

"I'd love to move to Queensland, but I know that means moving away from you."

He nodded and remained silent.

"You've just returned to Sydney and have an exciting

career ahead of you." She couldn't expect him to drop his career and follow her to an island resort.

"Cassie, I'll be honest with you." He looked her straight in the eye. "I'm not interested in a long-distance relationship."

The finality of his words shook her. If she moved to Queensland they'd be finished. No turning back.

She owed him the truth. "Neither am I. What sort of relationship are you looking for?"

He sipped his hot chocolate. "I look at Tim and Lisa and see how happy they are together. They love their kids and have created a wonderful family."

She agreed. "Their kids are great."

"I look at my parents, who will celebrate their thirty-fifth wedding anniversary next year."

"Wow, a big achievement."

He nodded. "Laura and Greg adore each other and can't wait to get married. How do you find a lasting relationship?"

"I think good communication helps. My parents never communicated effectively with each other and disagreed on all the important issues."

"Honesty is very important."

"I agree."

He leaned forward and sneaked a kiss on her lips.

Her heart melted like the warm and smooth chocolate milk in her mug. She didn't want this wonderful evening with Ryan to end.

The next morning Cassie struggled to climb the outdoor stairs. She reached the top and leaned back against the wall beside the front door of the holiday house.

Laura appeared in the doorway. "How's your ankle?"

"Improving. I've finished packing."

"Great. Is Ryan giving you a lift back to Sydney?"

She nodded. "We're planning to leave after lunch."

"That's our plan, too." Her sister gave her a hug. "I'm so excited that everything's working out between you two. Ryan has cooked up a big breakfast and I'd better get moving. The others are waiting for me in the car. We'll be back from our hike by lunchtime."

"Have fun." She waved goodbye to her sister. The delicious aroma of bacon and eggs tantalized her empty stomach as she limped down the hallway to the kitchen.

Ryan stood at the stove, adding tomato wedges to a frying pan. "I hope you're hungry. We can eat on the balcony."

"A great idea." She shuffled over to a stool at the breakfast bar.

Minutes later he served up two plates of food.

"You're spoiling me."

"You deserve to be spoiled." He added piping hot toast slices to their plates. "How's your foot?"

"Much better." She followed him outdoors and chose a chair facing the mountains.

He smiled. "The coffee is brewing. Would you like a cup now or later?"

"I don't mind—whatever is easier for you."

"I'll be back soon."

She poured a glass of orange juice and drank in the beauty of the mountains.

The cool breeze and warm sunshine invigorated her senses. The holiday house was situated on prime real estate and the large balcony overlooked the road and gardens. A number of people were out on the street jogging or walking their dogs.

He returned with two mugs of coffee. "Isn't the view stunning?"

She nodded. "If my ankle was better I'd take a stroll through the garden." A flight of steps from the balcony led down to the cottage garden.

She sampled her meal. "This is wonderful. Thanks for cooking breakfast."

"My pleasure. I cooked while the others got ready to go hiking."

The front door bell chimed.

Her stomach tightened. "Do you think it's Sean?"

"I'll go and see." He stood. "Do you want to see him?"

She nodded. "I want to find out what's going on."

"That's if he tells us the truth." His face hardened and his mouth formed a straight line.

She pressed her lips together. Tension exuded from his body. Sean would take one look at him and run if Ryan didn't calm down. "Can you give him a chance? Hear him out?"

"I'll try, but I'm not making any promises."

"Please, Ryan, he's reaching out to us. We need to listen to his side of the story."

He crossed his arms. "He'd better listen to a few things I have to say and not run away like last time."

"What are you going to do? Chain him to a chair?"

"Don't be ridiculous." He tapped his foot on the wooden decking.

She shook her head. "You can't make him stay and listen to you."

"If Sean wants my help then he'll listen to me."

The doorbell pealed again.

She frowned. "You'd better answer the door before whoever it is gives up and leaves."

He stomped inside and she placed her head in her hands, whispering a prayer.

Loud male voices echoed from the house.

She stood and hurried inside, each step on her injured foot shooting pain up her leg. Not far to go. She'd left her crutches in the apartment.

The voices from the front of the house abated. Had Sean left already?

Disappointment and anger raged inside her. If Ryan had

sent Sean away without giving him a chance, she'd have a few choice words to say.

She stumbled into the hallway and gasped. "Sean, what happened to you?"

Sean stared at the ceiling. "Can I come in?"

Ryan shoved his hands on his hips. "Do you want him coming in looking like this?"

She took in Sean's messy hair and disheveled clothes. "Where did you sleep last night?"

Sean stared at the floor. "It doesn't matter."

She sucked in a deep breath. "Ryan, he needs a shower and a change of clothes. Can we help him?"

Ryan paused. "If you insist."

"I do." She shot Ryan a stern look. "I'll hunt around the kitchen for something for him to eat."

"No, you go back outside and finish your breakfast that he has interrupted. I'll find some clean clothes and make him breakfast."

She attempted a smile. "Okay."

"Don't thank me yet." Ryan turned to face Sean. "You and I have a few things to discuss."

Bile rose in her stomach. This situation wasn't going to end well.

Ryan glared at Sean. "The bathroom is at the end of the hall."

Sean nodded. "Thanks."

Cassie took her weight off her injured ankle. "We'll talk soon." She limped away and disappeared into the kitchen.

"Get moving," Ryan said. "We haven't got all day."

Sean sent him a sour look. "I don't have a change of clothes with me."

"I'll find something for you." He kept a tight rein on his rising temper. Play it cool and focus on protecting Cassie from being hurt by Sean.

"Is Cassie okay? Did she hurt her foot?"

"Her ankle is getting better." He led Sean to a spacious bathroom and grabbed a towel from the linen cupboard. "There's soap and toiletries on the shelves under the basin and I'll be back in a minute with clothes."

Ryan walked into a nearby bedroom, unzipped his suitcase and pulled out clean clothes. No surprise his brother intended freeloading off him. He'd give him clothes but not cash. Would Sean ever get his act together?

He returned to the bathroom and handed the clothes to Sean. "They should fit you."

Sean nodded. "Thanks. Tell Cassie I won't be long."

Ryan grunted, leaving the bathroom before he said something he'd regret.

Cassie sat at the table on the balcony, finishing her breakfast. "Is he okay?"

He shrugged. "He didn't say much. I'll wait for him inside and make his breakfast."

"Do you think he'll run away?"

"I don't trust him." Who knew what stunt he'd pull next?

"I'll join you, and don't forget you need to finish your breakfast."

His stomach churned. "I've lost my appetite."

Cassie walked beside him to the kitchen and pulled out a stool at the breakfast bar, her brows drawn together.

He put bread in the toaster and paced the length of the hallway.

"Ryan," she called out.

"What?" He stopped at the entrance to the kitchen.

"You need to calm down."

He hid his clenched fists behind his back. How could she expect him to feel calm? "What I need is answers."

"You'll get them soon. I'll make your coffee."

"Thanks." He remained in the hall, keeping a close watch on the bathroom. He would get answers from his brother today, whether Sean liked it or not.

The toast popped up. Cassie poured the coffee and organized Sean's breakfast.

Ryan leaned against the kitchen door frame, arms crossed over his chest and his gaze glued to the bathroom door. The bathroom window was too small for Sean to escape through. He wouldn't put it past him to try and run again.

His brother emerged from the bathroom looking more respectable now that he'd cleaned up and put on fresh clothes.

"Where's Cassie?"

Ryan pointed to the kitchen. "In there."

Sean sauntered past and pulled out a stool beside her.

Ryan stood in the doorway, his temper rising at the familiar way Sean treated Cassie, as if they were still best friends. In contrast, his brother's eyes filled with contempt every time he darted a glance in Ryan's direction.

Cassie shifted her stool closer to Sean. "What's going on with you? I've been worried sick since your last phone call."

"I needed to see you."

She lifted a brow. "Why?"

Sean picked at the food on his plate. "I need your help."

Ryan stood over his brother. "Don't you dare ask her for money."

"I can ask for whatever I want. You don't control me."

He pointed to the door. "I think you should leave. Now."

Cassie placed her hand on Ryan's forearm. "Sean, please stay. And, Ryan, please calm down and hear him out."

Ryan drew in a deep breath. He stepped back and moved to the other side of the breakfast bar.

Cassie turned to Sean. "We can't help you unless you tell us the truth."

Ryan's frown deepened. "That's assuming he knows what the truth is."

"Ryan!" She shot him a stern look. "Be quiet and let Sean have his say."

He clenched his fists. "I'll shut up, but this had better be good. I don't want to listen to any more rubbish."

Sean finished his mouthful of toast. "I've really messed up this time."

How could it be worse than last time? What was worse than embezzling fifty thousand dollars?

"What happened?" she asked.

"I was doing okay, working for some guys I know and staying at their place."

Cassie nodded. "Where do they live?"

"It doesn't matter. I won't be there much longer."

"Why?" Ryan tapped his foot, his impatience growing. Had Sean done the wrong thing by these people?

Sean shrugged. "It's not working out."

"What sort of work were you doing?" Cassie asked.

"Nothing exciting. Mainly delivery work."

Ryan exploded. "You've been drug running?"

"No," Sean yelled. "It was legit work. They own a car spare parts business."

"Stolen spare parts?" he asked.

"Give me a break," Sean said. "It's all aboveboard."

Cassie's eyes begged him to back off. "Ryan, please let him talk."

"I don't think my questions are unreasonable. As far as I'm concerned my brother is capable of anything."

"I'm not a drug dealer."

Ryan sucked in another deep breath and counted to ten. He sipped his coffee, attempting to rein in his fury. "What's your problem?"

"I know someone who has been helping me out with a small cash flow problem."

He rolled his eyes. "Here we go. How much do you owe him?"

"Get off my case. Why do you always assume the worst?"

"Because I'm usually right."

Cassie flashed him a look. "Ryan, let him finish." She looked back at Sean and her voice softened. "Is that why you're concerned for your safety?"

"Cassie, don't fall for it. He'll give you a big sob story about how he's in danger and you must help him by lending him money. Isn't that right, Sean?"

Sean scowled. "I hate your superior, know-it-all attitude. Stop pretending that you want to help me. No one is buying it."

"Now you listen to me." Ryan's hands trembled, anger consuming his body. "How dare you interrupt our pleasant weekend with all your rubbish? Since you're so great, you can tell me why you haven't contacted Mom and Dad in over two years? Mom leaves a message on your cell phone every week."

"That's none of your business."

Ryan glared at his brother. "How can you treat our parents with such contempt after everything they've done for you?"

"You must be kidding. They do everything for you because you're their favorite son who can do no wrong."

Ryan shoved his hands on his hips. "That's no excuse for your behavior. I regret fixing your fifty-thousand-dollar mess. I thought I was helping you, but clearly I was wrong. I should have let you rot in jail."

"I didn't ask for your help," Sean said.

Ryan raised his voice. "You begged me to get that job for you at the company and this is how you thank me. When are you going to start repaying the fifty thousand dollars?"

Sean rubbed his hand over his unshaven jaw. "You're not listening to me. I have a cash flow problem and you're going to fix it for me."

"What? Are you out of your mind?"

"I need five thousand dollars by next week."

"I'm not giving you any money."

Cassie's eyes widened. "Sean, what have you done? Why do you need so much money?"

"It's a long story." Sean stood. "So, big brother, do you have your checkbook with you?"

"I'm not giving you another cent." How could his brother be so selfish and ungrateful?

Sean stepped closer to Cassie. "Can you help me out? I'm in a bind and I need to come up with this money fast."

She shook her head. "I'm sorry. I want to help you, but giving you money will just make everything worse."

"See, Sean, listen to Cassie. She agrees with me."

"Please, Cassie. I know I messed up but you're my last hope."

"Sean, I can't. You need to deal with your problems—"

"I thought I could count on you. Have you forgotten we were going to elope in Vegas?"

"Vegas." Ryan's anger intensified and he turned to Cassie. "Were you planning to marry my brother?"

Chapter 13

Cassie gasped, the full impact of Sean's words imploding in her mind. "Ryan, it's not true. I never wanted to marry Sean."

Ryan's cold gaze held her captive. "Why would he make up a story like this? Did you talk about going to Vegas?"

She bit her lip, unable to escape her past. "It was a stupid, drunken conversation not long before Sean disappeared."

"See, Ryan, I'm telling the truth." Sean stepped backward, edging toward the hall.

Ryan's gaze remained fixed on her. "Did you have a relationship with my brother?"

"No!" She rubbed her hands over her eyes. "We were good friends and spent a lot of time together. Sean was my only friend who wasn't judgmental about my drinking and he liked partying with me."

Ryan grunted. "Typical."

"I realize now that he enabled my addiction and our friendship wasn't healthy."

"What else are you hiding from me?"

Her stomach roiled, nausea threatening to overwhelm her. "You have to believe me. It was a silly conversation that meant nothing."

Ryan closed his eyes, stress exuding from his tense body. "I want to be able to trust you."

His words impaled her heart, cutting to her inner core. "You don't trust me."

He opened his eyes and let out a big breath. "I don't know what to think. Where did Sean go?"

She swung around, her mouth gaping open. "He's gone."

Ryan rushed past her. "I'm going to find him."

Ryan ran out of the holiday house and along the front path to the road. He stood beside the letter box, searching the tree-lined street for his brother. Where had Sean gone? His head start could only have been a couple of minutes.

He resisted the urge to smash his fist on the wooden fence. Unfamiliar feelings of jealousy had assaulted him at the thought of Cassie and his brother sharing a past relationship. Sean's insinuation had distracted Ryan, allowing his brother to make a quiet and quick escape.

He stomped back up the path, furious that Sean had once again avoided being held accountable for his behavior. Ryan detoured via the bedroom, grabbing his luggage. He paused in the doorway to the kitchen.

Cassie stood in the kitchen, her hands wrapped around a coffee mug. "Did you find Sean?"

He shook his head, his tone low and controlled. "I'm leaving."

Her downcast red-rimmed eyes met his gaze. "Why?"

"I need space, time to think."

"I'm really scared for Sean." She wiped a tear away from the corner of her eye. "I think something really bad is going to happen to him."

His wounded heart hardened, unable to deal with her misplaced empathy for his brother. "Greg and Laura can give you a lift home."

He walked out of the kitchen, each step taking him further away from the woman he loved. Her illogical loyalty to Sean spiked his anger. Could he trust her? He needed time away from Cassie to cool down and consider his next steps regarding the Sean situation. His brother was out of control and heading for disaster.

Cassie hugged a cushion as Ryan's footsteps pounded on the polished floorboards in the hallway.

Minutes later a door slammed. Silence. He was gone.

More tears flowed down her face. The man she loved had walked out on her. She didn't deserve his love.

Racking sobs shook her body, her tears soaking the cushion cover. Her past mistakes had driven him away.

She swiped tears from her eyes as she hopped over to the window, her ankle aching. Ryan's SUV was no longer parked on the drive.

She glanced at her watch. Laura and the others would be back in less than an hour. The last thing she wanted to do was answer a million questions about Ryan's early departure without her.

A bottle of red wine stood on the sideboard. Laura and Greg's engagement present from the restaurant owners last night.

She'd kill for a drink, anything to dull the pain. She grabbed the bottle and hurried to the kitchen. The throbbing in her ankle intensified, but she ignored it, desperate to locate a corkscrew.

Cassie rifled through the kitchen drawers and found an opener. She cradled the bottle in her hands. An expensive drop, it would glide down her throat and take away all her problems.

Her mouth watered. A glass. Did she need a glass?

No, just open the bottle, tip your head back and drink to the bottom like old times.

She picked up the corkscrew and reality hit her.

What was she thinking? Her gaze remained fixated on the bottle. It called her to open it.

Please, Lord, help me to walk away.

The bottle tormented her. Her mind whirled in different directions but she had to get away. Now.

Adrenaline pulsed through her and she turned her back on the bottle, stumbling toward the front door. Her ankle protested, but her mind screamed out louder.

She unlocked the door and threw the house keys on the table beside the door. Better to be locked out of the house so she couldn't return later and consume the bottle.

Hopping down the stairs, she used the railings for support. Each step took her further away from temptation.

She opened the apartment door, staggered inside and locked herself in before crashing on the sofa.

Tears poured down her face, relief mixed with sadness. That was close. Too close. Her weakness remained, even after all these months.

The comfortable one-bedroom apartment became her cozy cocoon. She dropped her head into her hands. How had it happened? Would her desire to drink ever disappear?

She whispered a prayer, thanking God for giving her the strength to walk away.

Her call to Julia's cell phone went straight to voice mail. She tried their home phone. No answer.

She curled up on the sofa and closed her eyes, imagining a life with Ryan minus the complication of her past. An impossible dream. Who would want to marry someone like her?

Next week she should hear if she was the successful applicant for the job in Queensland. Yesterday she had considered declining the position if they offered her the job.

What a difference a day made. Her whole outlook on her future had changed in a few short hours.

Julia and Ryan were right, though. The temptation to drink still haunted her and moving to Queensland might not be a smart decision. But she no longer had a compelling reason to stay in Sydney.

She dragged a pillow under her head. The emotional

drama of Sean's visit and her near fall into temptation had taken its toll.

Tears escaped from under her closed eyelids. Exhaustion overcame her and she dropped off to sleep.

The persistent knocking on the door dragged Cassie out of a dreamless sleep.

"Cassie, are you there?"

She struggled to her feet and unlocked the door.

Laura's jaw dropped. "What happened to you?"

"My life just fell apart."

"What? Where's Ryan?"

"He left."

"Why? What happened?"

She pressed her lips together. "It's a long story."

"I'm sorry." Laura embraced her in a big hug. "Do you want to tell me about it?"

"Okay. You can make coffee."

Laura busied herself making two mugs of coffee while Cassie filled her in with the skeleton details.

Her sister gave her another hug. "I had no idea Sean wanted a relationship with you."

"I'm not sure what Sean wanted. Even Sean doesn't know what he wants."

"It doesn't matter now—it's all in the past."

Cassie nibbled her lower lip. "I nearly drank your bottle of wine."

Laura sighed. "So that's why it's in the kitchen. You've had a stressful morning."

She nodded and wriggled into a more comfortable position on the sofa.

"But you didn't drink it." Laura sat beside her. "That's good. And Ryan will eventually calm down and see reason."

"I don't know if he will." Fresh tears formed in her eyes.

"He deserves someone better than me. Someone who doesn't have a past connection with his brother."

Laura frowned. "Do you really think Sean's in trouble? It's not just a big story to get your sympathy and money?"

"I know in my gut that this time he's on the level. He's desperate and I'm really worried about him."

"Is Ryan concerned, too?"

She sipped her coffee. "I think so."

"To be honest, I can't blame Ryan for being ticked off. Sean's track record for honesty isn't great."

"I know, but I can't shake the feeling that he's in danger. Call me crazy, but I'm frightened for him."

"You could always contact Sean and leave a message on his cell phone."

Cassie shook her head. "What good would it do? Ryan told Sean to stop harassing me for money. I doubt Sean would be game to contact me for fear of what Ryan would do if he found out."

"What would Ryan do?"

"Yell and rant at Sean again." She threw her hands in the air. "It's an impossible situation."

"You really think it's over for good between you and Ryan?"

Cassie nodded. "I love Ryan, but it's not enough. My past will always be a wedge between us."

On Wednesday afternoon Cassie rode the elevator to her father's office. They'd arranged to meet for lunch at a nearby restaurant before her father had called to say he'd be late. He'd asked her to meet him at his office.

She reached the top floor of the high-rise building. Her sensible low-heeled shoes sank into the plush carpet in the foyer and she inhaled the scent of fresh cut roses.

Her gaze darted to the left, homing in on Ryan's office at the end of the corridor. A part of her hoped she'd run into him. She missed seeing his face, hearing his voice.

Shaking her head, she turned right and headed to her father's office. Ryan hadn't contacted her since the disastrous weekend away, almost two weeks ago. She'd heard nothing from Sean, either. Was he still in trouble?

She'd see Ryan again at Laura and Greg's wedding.

Tears threatened and she bit her quivering lower lip. She needed to pull herself together and put Ryan out of her mind.

She entered her father's outer office, passing a vacant desk. *Dad's personal assistant must be at lunch.* She strolled through the open door into his private office and sat across from his desk.

Her father smiled and returned his attention to his phone call.

The magnificent view of the Sydney Harbour Bridge and Opera House snagged her attention. Nothing but the best was good enough for Dad.

He ended the phone call and sighed.

"Dad, are you okay? You sound breathless."

John slumped back in his chair. "I think so. I have chest pain."

"What? How bad?"

He paused and took a few deep breaths. "Comes and goes."

She leaned forward. "When did it start?"

"This morning."

"Why didn't you say something when you called earlier?"

"I didn't want to worry you over nothing."

She lifted a brow. "I don't think this is nothing."

"I'm fine." He stretched in his chair. "Ouch. My shoulder hurts, too."

She stood and rushed to her father's side. "You don't look fine to me."

"Who's not fine?" Ryan strode into the office.

"Something's wrong. He has chest pains."

John frowned. "You're overreacting." He tried to stand and fell back into his chair.

"Dad." She crouched beside him, reaching for his hand.

"I'm calling an ambulance," Ryan said.

She nodded. "Dad, you're sick."

John shook his head. "I'll be okay."

Her eyes filled with tears. Her father was never ill. He ate an appalling diet, but she'd always seen him as indestructible. "Try to breathe normally. The paramedics will be here soon."

Ryan hung up the phone. "They're minutes away. Cassie, do you know when his symptoms started?"

"This morning. He's breathless and has pain in his shoulder."

Her father's skin paled and fear squeezed her heart. "Dad, you're going to be okay. Hang in there."

"Cassie's right." Ryan crouched beside her. "Take some slow breaths. Help is on the way."

Pain lined her father's face, his hand resting on his chest.

Ryan's eyes widened. "Do you want me to pray for your dad?"

She nodded, closing her eyes and holding Ryan's hand.

"Lord, we pray the ambulance will arrive soon and the paramedics and doctors can help John. Amen."

"Amen and thank you."

Ryan's mouth curved upward and warmth filled his gaze. "You're welcome."

She let go of his hand, blinking away her tears.

Within minutes the paramedics arrived. Cassie stepped away from the desk, giving them room to work.

She called Laura on her cell phone.

Laura picked up on the third ring. "Hey, what's up?"

"Dad's sick. We called an ambulance and the paramedics are here."

"Slow down, you're not making sense," Laura said.

"Dad has chest pains."

"A heart attack?"

Her grip tightened on the phone. "Maybe."

"What's happening?" Laura's voice wavered.

"The paramedics are with him." She sucked in a deep breath. Now wasn't the time to lose it.

"Where are you?"

"Dad's office. I'll go to the hospital with him and you need to meet me there. Ryan's here with me."

"Which hospital?"

The paramedics placed her father on a stretcher.

"I've gotta go. Ryan can call you with the details."

She ended the call and turned to Ryan.

"I heard you," he said. "I'll call Laura."

"Thanks." She swiped at a tear rolling down her cheek.

Ryan placed his hand on her shoulder. "You need to go."

She nodded. "See you at the hospital?"

"Yes." He patted her arm. "He's in good hands."

Cassie followed her father's stretcher out of his office, her steps heavy. She waited for the elevator to arrive on their floor. What if her dad had been alone? How close had she come to losing him today?

The elevator doors closed, taking John and Cassie downstairs to the waiting ambulance. Ryan raced over to his office and grabbed his car keys. He called Laura on his cell phone, giving her the hospital details as he rushed to the elevator.

He tapped his foot, anxious for the elevator to arrive. John's condition worried him. A heart attack. How could this happen?

He prayed John had received medical attention early enough, before it was too late.

He hurried through the parking garage, wanting to be at the hospital with Cassie. Her distress had tugged at his battered heart. She'd reached out to him and he hoped he could help her through this ordeal.

He missed her, and seeing her teary blue eyes had torn him apart. Had Cassie seen or heard from Sean? Now that his anger had cooled he remembered her concern for his brother. She'd been adamant that Sean's life might be in danger.

John's health scare had shaken him up. What if he received a phone call about his brother being in the hospital? How would he react?

Was Sean in serious trouble or pulling another one of his stunts to get more money?

He dialed Sean's cell phone. The call went straight to voice mail. He waited, then left a message.

"Sean, it's Ryan. I've had time to think and I'd like to meet with you."

Ryan slipped his phone back into his suit pocket before leaping into his SUV.

The olive branch had been extended. What happened next was up to Sean, and he prayed his brother would do the right thing.

Chapter 14

Cassie pulled her chair closer to her father's hospital bed. She held his limp hand and attempted to smile. "You're going to be okay."

He nodded. "I'm all wired up." A cardiac monitor was set up beside his bed.

"Take it easy. The doctor will be back soon." She glanced at the clipboard in her lap. What did she know about Dad's medical history? When Laura arrived she could help her finish the paperwork.

A nurse returned to the tiny examination room. "We're ready to draw more blood and set up the ECG."

Cassie nodded, recognizing her cue to leave. Her father hated needles and, when the ambulance had arrived at the hospital, he'd demanded a private room. "Dad, I'll just be around the corner in the waiting room, fixing up your medical forms."

"Thanks." He squeezed her hand.

Tears pricked her eyes. "You're welcome." She kissed his forehead and left the room.

Cassie slid into a lumpy vinyl chair. The words on the forms blurred.

She closed her watery eyes. Laura and Ryan should be here soon.

The scent of Ryan's distinctive aftershave teased her senses. She opened her eyes.

Ryan dropped into the seat beside her. "How's he doing?"

"They're running tests and we should find out more soon."

"How are you holding up?"

She rubbed her hands over her face. "I'm okay."

"John will get better soon."

She nodded.

"But it's still a shock."

"I know. You think your parents are going to live forever and then something like this happens."

He frowned. "I didn't know John suffered from heart trouble."

"I don't think he knew, either, although the way he eats his cholesterol is probably sky-high."

He raised an eyebrow.

"You should see all the junk food in Dad's pantry. Laura and I have tried to get him to clean up his diet. Now maybe he'll listen to us."

"I hope so," he said.

The glass doors slid open and Laura rushed over to Cassie and hugged her tight. "Is there any news?"

"Not yet. Dad's lucky he came straight to hospital."

Her sister blinked away a few tears. "He's a fighter and he'll pull through." Laura gave Ryan a brief hug. "Thanks for being here with Cassie."

"No problem," he said. "I'm relieved John is going to be okay."

Laura nodded. "I called Mom and she said she'd be here ASAP. She wants us to call her when we know what's going on."

"Thanks for contacting her."

Laura ran her fingers through her brunette locks. "Can I go inside and see Dad?"

"Sure." Cassie passed the clipboard to her sister. "They need these forms completed. Dad's been grouchy about me seeing him undergo all the tests, but I know he'll want to see you."

"No problem. I'll keep that in mind." Laura disappeared into the examination room.

An elegant blonde woman approached Cassie. She looked to be in her late thirties, her eyes red and swollen.

"Hi, Ryan, and you must be Cassie, John's daughter," the woman said.

Cassie nodded and Ryan greeted her with a smile.

"I'm Debbie. Is John okay?"

Debbie? The woman Ryan had mentioned on the ferry. She shot Ryan a questioning look. "He's undergoing tests."

"What a relief." Debbie sighed. "I rushed over here as soon as I found out."

"Laura's with Dad in the examination room if you want to see him now."

Debbie shook her head. "I'll wait until later. I need to pull myself together first."

She nodded. Debbie's concern seemed genuine. Maybe she wasn't a gold digger after all.

"Cassie, it's great to finally meet you." Debbie wiped away a tear on her cheek. "Your father talks about you and Laura all the time."

"It's nice to meet you." What else could she say? Dad kept his personal life private and she'd only heard about Debbie through Ryan.

"If you'll both excuse me, I'm going to fix my makeup and find a cup of coffee. I'll be back later." Debbie spun around on her expensive heels and strode away.

Will Debbie return in time to meet Mom? Not a good idea. Cassie turned to Ryan. "Is she the Debbie you were talking about?"

He nodded. "I left a message for John's personal assistant and she must have contacted Debbie."

"She seems pleasant."

His eyes widened. "You like her?"

"She's older than I'd expected." She furrowed her brows. "I get the impression she has genuine feelings for Dad."

"John speaks very highly of her."

"Do you think they're serious?"

He shrugged. "That's a question for your father to answer."

Laura returned from the examination room. "The doctor wants to talk to us."

Cassie and Ryan followed Laura back into the room.

John lay in the bed with his eyes closed. He looked worn out.

Laura sat in the chair next to the bed.

"Your father's condition is stable," the doctor said.

Cassie let out a deep breath. "Is he going to make a full recovery?"

"We're optimistic and we'll know more when all the test results come in. It's good he came here early after the first sign of symptoms."

Laura shuddered. "I hate to think what might have happened if he'd stayed at the office."

They thanked the doctor and Cassie pulled up another chair next to Laura. Ryan stood back and leaned against the wall.

"Dad, you gave us a big scare today," Laura said.

"I know." John opened his eyes. "I had terrible pains in my chest and shoulder."

"It's okay, Dad," Laura said. "You need to rest and focus on recovering. Don't forget you have a daughter to walk down the aisle very soon."

"Sweetheart, I wouldn't miss your wedding for anything." He turned to Cassie. "We need to talk."

"Later," Cassie said. "You need to rest now."

"We must talk soon."

Laura pursed her lips. "Cassie can visit tomorrow and you can talk when you're stronger."

John looked at Cassie. "You promise?"

Cassie nodded. "I'll be back tomorrow."

He grabbed Cassie's hand. "Thanks. I'd planned to talk at lunch."

"I know." They had a lot to discuss and she hardly knew where to begin.

A knock sounded on the door. Her mom greeted them, passed on her best wishes to their father, and said she'd wait outside the tiny room.

What if Debbie showed up now? How would Mom cope? Would she cause a scene? Her father didn't need the stress.

"Dad, I need to go," Cassie said.

"Me, too," Ryan said. "John, I'll head back to the office and take care of things."

"Thanks, Ryan. Laura, can you stay?"

Laura nodded. "Greg will be here soon."

Cassie kissed her father's cheek before leaving the room with Ryan.

Outside the door, her mom gave her a warm hug. "You okay?"

"Yep." Cassie met Ryan's gaze. "Thanks for everything."

"No problem. Take care," he said, waving before walking away.

When would she see Ryan again? At the wedding? He'd been her rock today and she missed him.

She placed her hand on her mom's elbow. "Let's get out of here." Her gaze scanned the waiting room. No sign of Debbie. Relief consumed her. One less problem she'd have to handle.

They exited the hospital and Cassie slipped into the passenger seat of her mom's sedan.

Susan started the engine and reversed out of the parking spot. "I'm glad your father is okay."

"Did you want to visit him longer?"

She shook her head. "The nurse at the desk said they were limiting his visitors. I stayed out in the waiting room and I noticed a blonde woman hovering near the entrance to his room. Is she his girlfriend?"

"Yep." So far her mother seemed okay with this news. Why? "I met her for the first time this afternoon, although I'd heard about her through Ryan."

Susan frowned. "She looks young enough to be his daughter."

"I saw her before she fixed her makeup and she's older than you think. My guess is late thirties."

"Oh." She paused. "Your father hasn't let me know yet if he's bringing a date to the wedding."

"Check with Laura."

Susan nodded. "We need to finalize numbers soon."

Cassie stared at the stream of traffic up ahead. One question burned in her mind. She wanted to learn the truth. "What went wrong between you and Dad?"

"Everything. It's a long story."

"The traffic's heavy so we have plenty of time." She wanted answers from her mom. "Why has there been so much animosity between you two?"

"You really want to know?"

"I do. I'm trying to mend my relationship with Dad and wondering if you've got any insights that could be helpful."

Susan sighed. "Your father was never around when you and Laura were little. He's a workaholic and believed his role was to bring home a big fat paycheck. We grew apart and I resented his job, resented all the overseas trips, even though we could have gone, too."

"How come we didn't?"

"It's difficult traveling with small children. I felt lonely, isolated, trapped at home with all the parenting responsibilities. Most days your father left at dawn and came home after your bedtime."

Forgotten memories resurfaced. "I remember lying in bed, trying to stay awake until I heard Dad's car outside my bedroom window." Cassie pressed her lips together as hurt flared inside her and old insecurities lingered in her mind.

"It was impossible to put you girls to sleep. Those years were the hardest times of my life. Your father wasn't there for me and he couldn't understand why I was so needy."

Cassie shivered. "I also remember the fights between you and Dad." She'd hidden under her quilt with her baby doll to block out the yelling.

"I wish you'd never heard them." Susan sucked in a deep breath. "In hindsight I can see how damaging that was for you. Those last few months before we separated were the worst. I was angry and wanted him to feel my pain."

"Mom, I'm sorry."

"I felt like he only stayed because of you girls. He refused to do counseling, said he was too busy for such frivolous things. I decided to leave him because our marriage was beyond repair and you girls were suffering too much."

She raised an eyebrow. "But Dad moved out and I always thought he left us."

"I know." Her mom sighed. "I didn't correct your misconception because I didn't want you to hate me. I resented your father's inability to make you girls his priority. I blamed him for destroying our family and didn't make it easy for him to have access visits."

She frowned. "Mom, I had no idea."

"When your father briefly remarried, I made his life very difficult, which was wrong." She paused, staring straight ahead at the road. "It's taken me a long time to move on and too long to tell you the truth, but it's hard to face up to these things. I've always tried to be a good mother."

Cassie groaned. "It seems I've blamed Dad for a lot of things that weren't his fault."

"I'm so sorry. There's no excuse for what I did. Today I realized I had to tell you the truth. Please don't hate me."

"I could never hate you." She patted her mom's hand. "We all make mistakes. I forgive you."

Tears filled Susan's eyes. "Thank you. I want you to have the chance to fix your relationship with your father, and I didn't want him to die before you sorted out your issues with him."

"I'm seeing Dad tomorrow." Emotion choked her voice. "I think it's time I swallowed my pride and dealt with all the problems from the past."

"You mean Sean?"

She nodded. "Dad wanted to talk with me today over lunch, and I assume he wants to talk about Ryan and Sean."

"I hope it all goes well. You and Ryan seemed to be getting along fine at the hospital."

"I guess so."

"He cares about you. Maybe you two can work through your problems."

Cassie shook her head. "I think it's too late." She blinked away tears. "Sean and my past will always be an obstacle between us."

The next day Cassie located her father's private hospital room and peeked around the door. His eyes were closed and she hesitated in the doorway.

Her dad raised his arm. "Cassie, is that you?"

She walked into the room and sat beside his bed. "How are you feeling?"

"Alive. I've got aches and pains, but I'm doing okay."

She smiled. "I'm glad."

"I've had time to think."

"You gave us all a big scare yesterday."

He frowned. "For the first time in years I've stopped and taken stock of my life."

"Is that a good thing?"

"It's long overdue. Can we talk about Ryan and Sean?"

She nodded. "Another big mess I've made for myself."

"What happened?"

"Has Ryan spoken to you about the weekend at Katoomba?

"No." John sat up straighter in his bed. "I know Ryan cares about you and he's been moping around at work for the last week or more. Can't you both sit down and talk through your issues?"

"I wish it was that simple."

"Why isn't it?"

How could she explain herself in a way her father would understand? "Our values and outlook on life are different."

John frowned. "I don't understand."

"Take Sean, for example. Ryan believes Sean must be punished and make amends, and I want to see Sean recover from his problems."

"Ryan is right. Sean will never get his act together until he's made to face up to his actions and accept the consequences."

"But until Sean starts dealing with his current problems, he probably won't realize he's caused so much hurt and pain to others."

He raised an eyebrow. "Why do you believe that?"

"I've been there." She sighed. "It wasn't until I started to recover from my drinking problem that I realized how much pain and suffering I'd caused everyone." She sucked in a deep breath. "I'm sorry for all the pain I inflicted on you."

He nodded. "I've tried to be a good father to you and Laura, and I should have been around more when you were younger."

"It's okay. Mom explained that she didn't make it easy for you to see us."

"I could have pushed harder for visits." He rubbed his hand over his eyes. "I was busy with work and it was easier to back off than fight with your mother."

"I haven't made things easy for you." Shame filled her

heart as she recalled her behavior during their argument over Sean.

He frowned. "In many ways I blamed myself for your drinking problem. You're right in thinking you're different from my mother. Her denial of her drinking problem made life difficult for the whole family."

"I've been sober for nearly two years, and I'm sorry Grandma's drinking turned you away from God."

"I'm sorry I've been so hard on you." He reached for her hand. "I can see you've changed, and maybe you're right in thinking your faith has made a difference."

She squeezed his hand. "It's true, Dad. God's real and He loves us."

He shrugged. "I'll think about it."

She inhaled a deep breath, hope filling her heart. "I'm sorry about all the stuff that happened in the past with Sean. Can you forgive me for all the terrible things I said to you back then?"

He nodded. "I should be the one asking for forgiveness. I could have been more understanding of your situation."

"Dad, I forgive you. I want to wipe the slate clean and start over."

"I love you and Laura, and I want to see my girls happy. Laura has Greg and I'm hoping you and Ryan can sort things out."

"I don't think it's going to happen."

"Do you love Ryan?"

She nodded, moisture threatening to invade her eyes.

"Then go fix it. I wish I'd done marriage counseling with your mother and worked on saving our marriage."

She lifted a brow. "You still care for Mom?"

"She was a big part of my life and we share two wonderful daughters." He sighed. "Don't make the same mistakes I made. Fight for Ryan. He's a good man, and I think he'd make an excellent husband."

She blinked away a few tears. "By the way, I heard about the Queensland job."

"They offered you the job?"

"Yes, a few days ago."

"Have you accepted their offer?"

"Not yet. I haven't even told Mom and Laura that I'm the successful applicant. They're both too upset at the thought of me leaving Sydney."

"What are you going to do?"

"I don't know. Before things blew up with Ryan I'd been thinking about declining the offer."

"But now you're not so sure."

She nodded. "I can't expect Ryan to move to Queensland. But now I don't have a big reason to turn down the job."

"What if I gave you a reason?"

"Oh, Dad, my relationship with Ryan is beyond hope. I can't see how you talking to him would make a difference."

He shook his head. "That's not what I'm thinking."

"Then what are you proposing?"

"A job offer at a hotel I plan to redevelop."

She widened her eyes. "You're serious?"

He nodded. "The position is yours if you want it."

Chapter 15

Cassie opened her mouth, but no words came out. Her father had offered her a job. She hadn't seen this coming.

John smiled. "So, what do you think?"

"Umm, where's the hotel?"

"Sunshine Coast."

Queensland. Her dream location. "Tell me more."

"A few months ago I decided to diversify my investment portfolio."

She nodded. "A smart plan."

"I looked at hotels and resorts that could be revamped and had potential for expansion. I found a unique property in a great location. It's a small hotel with lots of land and only a short walk to the beach."

"So you bought it."

"And got it for a good price. The permits are in place to do significant renovations."

"Congratulations." She smiled. "I hope it turns out to be a good investment. Where do I fit in?"

"I'd like you to run the resort."

Her heart skipped a beat. "Me? You'd trust me to manage your resort?"

"Absolutely. A while back you said you needed a new challenge, and this project would be perfect for you."

"You really want me to be the resort manager?"

He grinned. "You'll be the boss. At first you'll be managing a small hotel operation, but after the renovations are completed you'll be heading up a first-class luxury resort."

Her jaw dropped. "Dad, I don't know what to say."

"Say no to the other job and yes to me. I promise you the job will be challenging."

No doubt. A massive upward career move. "You really think I can do it?"

"You've got the right qualifications, and I'll provide you with an excellent remuneration package."

"I'm stunned you have so much faith in my abilities."

"I believe in you, and I also believe you're the right person for this job. I'm hoping you'll accept my offer."

What did she have to lose? Now Ryan was out of the picture, she had nothing to hold her back.

"I accept." She leaned over and hugged her dad. "Thanks for believing in me."

"You do realize you'll be working long hours and it won't be a walk in the park."

She nodded. "When do you want me to start?"

"After Laura's wedding. The purchase will be finalized over the next few weeks."

"Sounds wonderful. I'm so excited. Thanks so much for giving me this incredible opportunity."

"My pleasure. I know you'll do a great job."

His approval warmed her heart. One more question lingered in her mind. "I met Debbie yesterday. Is she your girlfriend?"

He nodded. "I'm sorry you two had to meet under these circumstances. I was going to introduce you to Debbie this weekend."

"Is your relationship serious?"

"Not yet. We've been seeing each other for a while. I'd like to bring her to Laura's wedding, but I'm not sure how your mother will react."

"She'll cope. She'll be more upset at the thought of me moving to Queensland than you bringing a date."

"You need to tell her sooner rather than later."

She nibbled her lower lip. "I'll tell Mom and Laura tomorrow at dinner."

"They'll be happy for you."

"Once they've calmed down and recovered from the shock. Laura's not going to be happy with you."

"She'll get over it soon enough. When are you going to tell Ryan?"

She shrugged. "I guess he'll hear through Laura. I won't be seeing him until the wedding."

"You can't call him?"

"What's the point? I'll be leaving Sydney soon for a new life in Queensland."

Cassie closed the door to her apartment, flung her keys on the side table and collapsed on the sofa.

Julia wandered into the living room. "How did your hospital visit go?"

"Really well. You'll never believe what happened. I feel so blessed."

Julia smiled. "You patched things up with Ryan. I'm so happy for you, and I'd hoped you two would end up together—"

"No, I haven't seen Ryan today."

"Oh, I'm sorry. I thought only Ryan could put a smile that big on your face."

"It's my dad. He bought a hotel on the Sunshine Coast to renovate into a luxury resort and he wants me to run it."

"Wow, that's incredible." Julia grinned. "Did you have any idea he was planning this?"

Cassie shook her head. "He took me completely by surprise. We talked about a whole lot of other stuff and our relationship is in a much better place."

"I'm so excited for you. Did you accept his job offer?"

"I sure did." The reality of her new life started to sink in.

"When will you start?"

"After the wedding."

Julia sat beside her on the sofa. "I'm going to miss you."

"I'll miss you, too, but we can still catch up by phone and email."

"And I'll be expecting an invitation to the grand opening of your resort. I quite like the idea of a weekend away at a luxury resort."

"Absolutely. You'll have to stay for a week."

"What about Ryan? Does he know about your new job?"

She shook her head. "I'll tell Mom and Laura tomorrow night at dinner, and I guess he'll find out through Laura and Greg."

"You could always call him."

"He made his feelings very clear during the weekend away. Yesterday didn't change anything."

"Did he mention Sean?"

She shook her head. "Ryan was a great help and he prayed with me while we waited for the ambulance."

"A good sign."

"I think he has rediscovered his faith, but it's too late for us."

"Why? Has he told you he doesn't want to see you again?"

"No, but too much has happened and I can't erase or change my past." If Ryan couldn't accept her history and trust her, their relationship was doomed. "I do have good news. I met Dad's girlfriend yesterday."

"Really? What's she like?"

"She seems nice. Dad's planning to bring her to the wedding."

"You really did have a big, deep and meaningful with your father."

"His health scare has mellowed him a bit. I don't know—maybe he'll be back to his old self in a few days' time and driving me crazy again."

"I hope not. I'm looking forward to meeting your new and improved father."

Cassie laughed. "I feel like a weight has been lifted off my shoulders. I'm about to start a new and exciting life."

"I think you'll miss Ryan."

Tears pricked her eyes. "I miss him every day, but what can I do? I haven't heard from Sean, either."

"Do you think Ryan has contacted Sean?"

"Who knows? With Sean I often think no news is good news."

"Are you going to contact Sean?"

She nodded. "After Laura's wedding I'll let him know that I'm moving and make sure he has Ryan's phone number."

"Would Sean contact Ryan if he's in trouble?"

"I hope so, and I want to believe Ryan would help him because he's that type of guy—loyal and dependable."

If only Ryan was *her* guy. She shifted her foot up onto a stool. The pain from the sprain had receded. In contrast, her pain over Ryan's decision to leave her during their weekend away grew stronger every day.

Her upcoming move to Queensland should help her get over him. A new environment with no reminders of Ryan and what could have been if circumstances had been different.

A week later Ryan sat at his desk, analyzing six-figure amounts on a spreadsheet. Something didn't add up. The project was way over the estimated budget, and he needed to wade back through the figures to locate the problem.

He glanced at the time on his computer screen. Twenty minutes past two and he hadn't stopped for a lunch break. The coffee his personal assistant had brewed up a few hours ago was cold and half drunk on his desk.

John had been in the hospital for a few days and was

now resting at home. Ryan had put in long hours to keep on top of everything at the office.

He highlighted a costing figure that looked inflated in the spreadsheet. The phone rang and he picked up the handset. “Ryan Mitchell.”

“Ryan, it’s…umm, Sean.”

“Hey, are you okay?”

“I need you to—*ouch*—come get me.”

His grip tightened on the handset. “Where are you? What happened?” Sean sounded terrible.

“Some guys beat me up.” He paused. “I’m at the end of your street near the Italian café on the corner.”

“I’m on my way.”

Ryan shut down his computer and scrawled a note for his personal assistant.

Adrenaline rushed through him as he waited for the elevator to take him to the ground floor. He was tempted to take the stairs, but eighteen flights would take longer than waiting for the elevator.

Was Sean okay? Why had those guys beaten him up? A random attack or something more sinister?

He suspected his brother knew his assailants and owed them money. Would this nightmare ever end?

Sean probably needed medical attention. Had an ambulance been called? He’d contact his parents after he knew what was going on. No need to worry them unnecessarily.

The elevator door opened and he stepped into the empty space. The downward journey seemed to take forever.

The door slid open. He rushed out of the building and headed down the street, spotting a crowd near the café on the corner.

He approached the group and found his brother sprawled out on the ground. “Sean.”

An older lady turned to face him. “Are you Ryan, his brother?”

He nodded. "What happened?" Blood covered Sean's face and his arm rested at an awkward angle.

"It all happened so fast." The woman's voice shook. "A car stopped at the light and three men jumped out. Two of them grabbed him and the other one punched him in the face and stomach. Then they threw him aside, got back in the car and sped off."

Ryan kneeled next to his brother. "Are you okay? Can you move?"

Sean nodded. "My head and arm hurt."

"Did someone call an ambulance?"

The lady shook her head. "He insisted we wait for you. The men were driving a black sedan, but no one remembers the car plates."

Ryan turned to Sean. "Do you want to go to hospital by ambulance or with me?"

"With you," Sean said. "No ambulance."

Ryan frowned. "My car is in the parking garage. I'll be back here in a few minutes to take you to the ER." He looked up at the lady. "Can you stay with him until then?"

She nodded. "He hit his head hard when they threw him to the ground and his shoulder might be dislocated."

"Okay. I won't be long."

"Thanks," Sean whispered.

Ryan ran back to his office building. He checked his suit pocket, thankful his keys and wallet were tucked inside. No time to grab his phone. He opened the parking garage door and raced down the ramp to his SUV.

He revved the engine and drove out of the car park, stopping at the corner. He flicked on the hazard lights before racing over to Sean.

His brother sat up, holding his injured arm. The bleeding from his nose had eased.

"I'll help you up," Ryan said. "We'll take it slow."

Another man stood on the other side of Sean and together they eased him to his feet. Car horns blared and traffic backed up behind Ryan's SUV.

Ryan ignored the traffic as he helped Sean limp over to the car and crawl into the reclined passenger seat.

He thanked the onlookers and jumped into the driver's seat, waiting for the lights to change to green.

He glanced at his brother. "Are you comfortable?"

"Sort of." Sean held a handkerchief up near his face.

"You know we should have called an ambulance."

Sean frowned. "I don't have ambulance insurance."

"I could have paid for it."

"You've paid out too much for me already. The ER is covered by Medicare and I'm not hurt too bad."

He nodded. "We'll be there soon." Since when had Sean been concerned about spending his money?

His brother's attitude seemed different, somehow. More thankful instead of demanding and rude—a positive sign.

He pulled up outside the ER and helped his brother walk inside. The hospital staff took down Sean's details while Ryan went out to move his car. When Ryan came back in, Sean was in a curtained-off exam area.

Before long a doctor came to examine Sean. He prescribed pain meds and ordered X-rays for Sean's arm.

Ryan stood back and the medical team took over. At last they all left the curtained cubicle and he was alone with his brother.

He dropped into a seat beside Sean's bed. "How are you doing?"

Sean groaned. "My arm hurts real bad, my head hurts and my stomach's queasy."

"Mild concussion and a suspected broken arm would do that to you. At least your nose isn't broken."

"It feels like it's broken. How long have we been here?"

Ryan glanced at his watch. "About two hours. I'll call Mom and Dad soon. They'll want to come down and see you—"

"No, I don't want them to see me like this. Please don't tell them."

"I can't keep this from them." Ryan drew in a deep breath. "You're their son and despite everything they love you."

Tears filled Sean's eyes. "I'm a mess and I don't want to face them."

"Tell them you're sorry, that is if you *are* sorry for all the pain you've caused them."

Sean nodded, tears rolling down his swollen cheeks. "I've screwed up big-time. I got in so deep I couldn't find a way out."

"Do you know the people who beat you up?"

He shook his head. "But I know who ordered the beating because I ran out of time to pay the five grand."

Ryan frowned. Cassie had been right all along.

Pangs of guilt shot through him. If he'd tried harder to help his brother a few weeks ago, maybe he wouldn't be in a hospital bed right now.

It was pointless to second-guess what might have been. Had this happened to Sean so he'd realize he needed help?

"Are you filing a police report?" Ryan asked.

Sean shook his head. "I'd rather forget this ever happened."

"What about the money? Will these people attack you again?"

"I guess so. I need to disappear, go someplace where they can't find me."

"You're not going anywhere until you've seen Mom and Dad. They're beside themselves with worry."

"Do you want them to see me looking like this?"

"You need to face Mom and Dad, and you need to honor all your debts."

"My head hurts. Can we talk about this later?"

"No." Frustration coursed through him. "We should have talked about this long before now."

"I want to see Cassie. Can you call her and get her to come here?"

Ryan cleared his throat, quelling the raw emotion that threatened to enter his voice. "Why? You'll see Cassie, but you won't see your own parents?"

Sean sighed. "If we have to talk about this now, then I want Cassie here. I'll see Mom and Dad after."

It would take his parents at least three or four hours to get here. Of all the people Sean wanted to see, why did it have to be Cassie?

Greg had told him a few days ago that Cassie was moving to Queensland to run John's new hotel redevelopment. Within weeks she'd be leaving Sydney and leaving him for good.

He couldn't keep Cassie out of his mind, no matter how hard he tried. He should have contacted her last week. Instead, he kept putting off calling her, using the excuse that he had too much work on at the office. The possibility of a future with Cassie looked bleak.

"Okay, I'll call Cassie, then I'll contact Mom and Dad. I left my phone at the office and I'll need to find a pay phone."

"Can you warn them that I'm not looking too good?"

He nodded. "You've outdone yourself with two black eyes."

"Those guys were professional thugs. One hit to my face has smashed it to pieces."

"It could have been worse." What if the street hadn't been busy with the lunchtime crowd? Would they have stayed longer and beaten him to death?

Ryan stood. "I'll be back soon." He turned to walk out of the room.

"Ryan."

He spun around. "Yeah."

"Thanks, bro."

"Sure." *Wow.* Sean had thanked him! Had he heard right?

"I know you're angry with me and you didn't have to help me."

Ryan rubbed his hand through his hair. "You're my brother. How can I turn my back on you?"

"I've been a rotten brother and I don't deserve your help."

"I've been talking a lot to Cassie's pastor over the last month."

"Have you gone religious like Cassie?"

He nodded. "I've discovered that no one deserves to be forgiven, and we can't earn God's love. We all make mistakes and I need to learn how to forgive and move on."

Sean paused. "I'm sorry about everything, and I'm not just saying that because you helped me earlier."

"I get that now. Please let Mom and Dad back into your life. They love you so much."

Sean blinked away his tears. "I know. I've failed them and I hate the fact I keep disappointing them."

"You can't avoid Mom and Dad forever. The longer you stay away, the worse it will be."

"I'll see them tonight." He wiped his eyes. "How long will I be here?"

"Your arm should be x-rayed soon. I'll stay until Cassie and our parents arrive."

Sean nodded and closed his eyes.

Ryan walked outside into the busy corridor. He located a pay phone in the waiting room. An elderly lady sat in a chair beside the phone, deep in conversation.

He leaned back against the wall and waited his turn. Cassie's cell phone number was stuck in his memory. He loved her and missed her.

During the past few hours he'd received a revelation. Cassie's perspective on Sean and his potential road to recovery made sense. The doctor had spoken to him privately about Sean's gambling problem. The hospital had a ward that his brother could be transferred to tonight, if Sean was willing to cooperate.

Ryan hoped Cassie could come to the hospital straightaway. He looked forward to seeing her and prayed she'd give him a second chance.

Chapter 16

The pedestrian traffic light turned red and Cassie stopped at the curb opposite Circular Quay. Cars and buses streamed past her as the city bustled with late-afternoon traffic. Her ferry departed for Manly Wharf in fifteen minutes.

Her cell phone chimed in her purse. Private number. She answered the call. “Hello.”

“Hi, Cassie, it’s Ryan.” Tension echoed in his voice.

“Oh, hi. What’s up?”

“Sean’s in the hospital and he wants to see you.”

“Is he okay? What happened?”

“Some thugs beat him up. He’s got a concussion and probably a broken arm.”

She gasped. “Does he know who did it?”

“Yeah, and he owes five grand to the guy they work for.”

She chewed on her lower lip. “I’m on my way. Which hospital?”

Ryan provided the details and Cassie ended the call. She headed back toward the hotel, scanning the traffic for a vacant cab.

She walked to the closest bus stop. Where were the cabs? A bus might be the fastest way to travel the short distance to the inner-city hospital.

Lord, thank You for protecting Sean from more serious injuries. I’m glad he contacted Ryan and I pray they’re getting on okay.

Cassie hopped on a crowded bus and stood in the aisle.

She gripped the handrail as the bus stopped and started up the congested street.

Why did Sean want to see her? She assumed Ryan was at the hospital because Sean had contacted him.

Her heart broke over Sean's situation. He desperately needed help before it was too late. Was this beating a wake-up call for him? Would it make him realize his life was a mess and he needed professional help?

Before long the bus stopped outside the entrance to the busy hospital. Cassie located the ER, and the lady at the reception desk gave her Sean's room number.

The curtain around Sean's cubicle was partly open. She stood in the doorway, watching the brothers. Ryan sat beside Sean and they appeared engrossed in their conversation.

Cassie stepped inside the room, and Ryan gave her a toe-tingling smile.

She pressed her lips together. "I'm here."

"That was fast," Ryan said.

"I was at the quay when you called."

She walked over to the bed and pulled up a chair on the side opposite Ryan. Sean had two black eyes and a bandaged nose. "Sean, you look awful."

"This isn't my finest hour."

"What happened? Ryan said some guys beat you up."

He nodded. "I owed them money and didn't pay up in time."

"What are you going to do? Have you got the money to pay them?"

"Nope and I've gotta get out of here, disappear for a while."

She frowned. "Running away didn't fix your problems last time."

"I don't have a choice. These guys will be back, and I'm scared about what might happen next time."

Ryan stood. "Do you want to spend the rest of your life

on the run, looking over your shoulder and wondering when your past will catch up with you?"

He shook his head. "I don't have the cash and they'll be back to get me. I need to disappear for a long time."

"There's another way," Ryan said, sitting back in his chair.

Cassie met Ryan's gaze. She missed his warm looks and heart-stopping smiles.

Ryan switched his attention to Sean. "I think it's time you started dealing with your problems."

"You can't make me go to rehab."

"I know, but if you want to get your life back on track then it's a good option."

She nodded. "Ryan's right. I managed to overcome my problems and you can do it, too, if you really want to."

"It's not a short-term quick fix and there are some excellent programs available that run for several months."

"I don't know." Sean's eyes widened. "I need to get out of here real soon. When can I get discharged?"

She moved closer to the bed and placed her hand over Sean's. "It'll be a tough ride, but we can help you through this."

Ryan nodded. "Your doctor told me there's a rehab unit in the hospital. They have a bed available, if you want it."

"Please, Sean, this is your fork in the road," Cassie said. "One of the most important decisions you'll make in your life." She held his hand. "You can beat this and we can help you beat it."

Sean closed his eyes. "I gotta get out of here."

"Mom and Dad will be here soon, and you promised me if Cassie was here you'd see them."

Tears escaped from Sean's eyes. "I'm scared that I'm not strong enough to do this."

"Think about the alternative," Ryan said. "Do you want to be beaten up again?"

"If you work a program, you'll be off the streets and safe for a few months," she said.

"The staff will look after you and help you to rebuild your life. There's a program located near the beach, not far from where I live, and I'll be able to visit you," Ryan said.

"That sounds like a good plan." She smiled. "Your parents could drive down and visit, too."

Sean opened his eyes and sucked in a deep breath. "Cassie, do you think I can do it?"

She nodded. "And so does Ryan."

"I sure do. It's your best option."

"Actually, it's your only good option," Cassie said. "When you recover you'll thank us for convincing you to take this step."

"Okay," Sean conceded. "I'll give it a try. But if it doesn't work—"

"Don't say that," she said. "It will work. Every day I'll be praying for you."

"What about the money?" Sean asked.

Ryan frowned. "We'll work something out. All you need to think about is getting better."

A nurse entered the room. "It's time for your arm to be x-rayed."

Ryan stood. "Cassie, would you like to have coffee?"

"Yes, please," she said. "We'll be back soon."

The nurse nodded. "He'll be away for at least half an hour, maybe an hour."

Cassie followed Ryan out of the room.

"There's a café next to the main entrance," she said.

"Okay, let's go."

She walked beside him along the corridor. "I can't believe he has agreed to go into rehab."

"God has answered our prayers."

She glanced up at him. "Have you been praying a lot for Sean?"

He nodded. "I have faith that God will help my brother

conquer his problems, and I know I need to forgive Sean for a whole lot of stuff."

She stopped walking, stunned by his words. "Does this mean you understand why I want to forgive Sean?"

His smile lit up his eyes. "I think so."

Wow. He shared her faith, and she struggled to contain her joy. "I guess we've got a whole lot of stuff to talk about over coffee."

"Yep." He reached for her hand.

She tucked it in his and strolled with him to the café.

His gray eyes sparkled. "Are you hungry?"

She perused the menu. "A burger with a side salad will do me."

"Same here, but I'll have a side of fries."

They placed their orders at the counter and found a quiet table in the corner.

She wriggled into a more comfortable position in her wooden chair. "What happened? Did Sean phone you?"

He filled her in with the details.

"I can't believe they beat him up in broad daylight on a busy city street."

"These guys must be professional thugs. I hate to think how my brother got caught up with them."

"No wonder he's scared. He's fortunate he wasn't more seriously hurt."

"During his initial medical assessment he admitted to the staff that he has a gambling problem. One of the doctors spoke to me about the short-term rehab clinic in the hospital."

"So he can transfer to the clinic tonight and move to a longer-term rehab program soon?"

He nodded. "But it's important he voluntarily agrees to go. After we eat, I'll talk to the staff and sort out the paperwork."

A waiter arrived with their drinks.

She sipped her latte. "What time are your parents due?"

"In about three hours. I'll wait here at the hospital for them, and they'll stay at my place for at least a few days."

"How did they react to the news?"

"They're shocked but relieved that Sean has agreed to seek help."

"What about the five grand?"

He frowned. "I'll talk to my lawyer about how to deal with that particular problem."

A waiter placed their burgers on the table.

Her stomach rumbled. Lunch had been a long time ago. "May I say grace?"

He nodded and closed his eyes.

"Lord, please bless this food. We're thankful Sean's safe and we pray he'll work the programs and recover fully from his problems. Amen."

"Amen," he said.

She smiled. "I assume you've been seeing Simon a lot."

"I've been attending the Sunday morning service."

"Really?" She took a bite from her cheeseburger.

He laughed. "I've been meeting with Simon and a couple other guys for breakfast before the service, and they've helped me understand a few things. I'm sorry I gave you a hard time over my brother." He met her gaze, warmth emanating from his eyes. "Please forgive me."

"I forgive you." *Lord, thank You for answering my prayers.*

They chatted about church and the things he'd been learning. He polished off his burger and wiped his mouth, then turned serious. "So where does this leave us?"

She lowered her gaze, picking at her salad. "You were right about the resort job."

"What do you mean?"

"I'm a recovering alcoholic, and I'm always going to have a weakness in that area." She pressed her lips together. "I thought I could get over the temptation, be strong enough to never fall off the wagon, but it's not true."

"Cassie, I understand—"

"Do you, really? This will be a lifelong struggle for me because I'm tempted to drink when I'm stressed or something bad happens."

He let out a slow breath. "I want to help you and support you."

"My life is complicated." She held his gaze. "I'm not proud of a lot of things I've done in the past."

"I can't claim to have a perfect past, either. What matters is the present and where we can go from here."

She twisted her hands together in her lap. "We need to talk about a few things." Like the fact she had committed to moving to Queensland in a few months.

"Do you want to take a walk through the gardens?"

She nodded. "Thanks for dinner."

"My pleasure." He glanced at his watch. "We've got time before Sean's due back in the ward."

She placed her hand in his and walked outside into the rose garden. Fairy lights lit up the enclosed area and bench seats were positioned along the winding paths.

"Cassie, I'm sorry I walked out on you at the holiday house."

She stopped and faced him. "You were angry."

"Sean's behavior was the final straw. I needed space to think and deal with stuff. I also know Sean brought up the Vegas thing as a decoy."

"Yep. He successfully distracted us and made his escape."

He nodded. "I'm thankful God brought you into my life. Your faith challenged me to look at my life. My priorities have changed."

She walked beside him along the path. "I'm so happy you and Sean are on the way to rebuilding your relationship."

"When I saw Sean injured by the side of the road, I realized he needed my help. I finally understood the prodigal son parable."

"I know what you mean. Dad being sick in the hospital gave me a big wake-up call. What if he had died before I had a chance to mend our relationship?"

"There's nothing like the prospect of death to shake us up."

She nodded. "I realized my prejudices against my father had clouded my judgment. I obsessed about all the bad things and ignored the good."

"Like me with Sean. All I saw were problems. I didn't acknowledge his potential to grow and change into a better person."

"You know, I spent years trying to gain Dad's approval." She paused beside a fountain. "I learned the hard way that God's approval is what matters and, in the end, Dad proved he had more faith in me than I'd ever imagined."

Ryan took hold of her other hand and gazed into her eyes. "Cassie, will you give me another chance? I can't promise I'll always do the right thing because I'm far from perfect. But, I can promise to love you."

Her heart melted. He loved her and wanted to be with her, even after everything that had happened.

She threw herself into his arms, snuggling her head against his broad chest.

"Oh, Ryan, I love you so much."

He tilted her chin and his mouth enveloped hers in an emotion-charged kiss.

She wound her arms around his neck and deepened the kiss, reveling in his closeness. This was where she belonged.

He raised his head and brushed a lock of hair off her forehead. "I love you, Cassandra Beaumont, and I'd like to have the privilege of spending the rest of my life with you."

"I love you, Ryan Mitchell." She gazed into his eyes. "I

want to wipe the slate clean and start over." She reached up and sealed the deal with a kiss.

He stepped back, concern shadowing his face. "Are you sure there isn't something you've forgotten to tell me?"

She lifted a brow. "Oh, you know about my job?"

"Had you forgotten?"

"Only momentarily, I'm a little distracted."

"Hmm. I could distract you further." He kissed the tip of her nose.

"That wouldn't be hard." She weaved her fingers through his hair.

"What's the deal with your job?"

The job. She switched her brain into gear. "I'm moving to Queensland after Laura and Greg's wedding. Yesterday I visited Dad and signed my employment contract."

"I thought his doctor had ordered him to rest."

"He can't help himself, and this new venture is separate from the main company."

"So, what are we going to do?"

She frowned. "I love you, and I don't want to live a thousand miles away from you."

"Me, neither." He traced his finger along the curve of her cheek.

She wrapped her arms around him. "We'll have to pray about it. I'm sure God has it all worked out."

Chapter 17

Cassie wriggled her toes in the sand on Manly Beach and Ryan draped his arm around her waist. The flash from the camera brought a smile to her lips.

Laura held up the skirt of her bridal gown. "These photos had better be good because the sand will ruin my dress."

Greg laughed, picked up his bride and carried her further up the beach. The photographer positioned them for more photos.

Ryan held Cassie's hand and whispered in her ear. "Let's go for a walk along the beach."

"Why?" She tipped her head to the side. "What if the photographer needs us?"

"I already checked, and I can steal you away for a short time. We can walk on the sand toward North Steyne, where there are fewer people around."

"Sure." She left her shoes behind and fell into step beside him, hitching up the skirt of her silk bridesmaid dress. The midday sun warmed her bare arms. Waves rolled into the shore, the salty foam creating ripples on the firm golden sand.

Ryan led her to a secluded section of the beach. A group of surfers were catching the breaking waves out in the deeper water.

He drew her into his arms, raising her chin with his thumb. "I've made plans tonight for a romantic dinner overlooking the beach."

Her heart danced to a faster beat.

He reached into an inner pocket in his jacket, removing a small navy blue velvet box.

She inhaled a few sharp breaths, her heart overflowing with love for the man holding her hand.

He dropped down on one knee in the soft, dry sand, his warm eyes capturing her gaze.

"Cassie, I love you with my whole heart." He opened the box, revealing a sparkling sapphire-and-diamond engagement ring.

She gasped. "It's stunning."

He nodded. "I want to spend the rest of my life with you, grow old with you. Will you do me the incredible honor of marrying me and becoming my beautiful wife?"

"Yes." She blinked away tears. "I love you, and I want to marry you as soon as possible."

"A fabulous plan." His gentle hands slipped the ring on her finger, the sunlight catching the sapphire facets surrounded by diamonds. He stood up and took her in his arms.

"Wow, it's perfect."

"I'm glad you like it." He trailed his fingertip along her cheek, and lowered his head.

His soft lips teased hers, enticing her to deepen the kiss. She closed her eyes and parted her lips, welcoming his sweet embrace.

Moments later he pulled back, his gaze intense. "We need to set a date. Soon."

Cassie nodded and raised her hand, admiring her engagement ring. Ryan had spared no expense.

"You can't keep your eyes off your ring."

"It's beautiful, and it represents our love."

"Why don't we have a small, intimate wedding soon, and have a big celebration when we launch the new resort?"

"But the resort might not be ready for months." She smoothed the skirt of her dress.

"Since I'll be managing the redevelopment, I can assure you the project will run on schedule."

She met his warm gaze. "I'm so glad you accepted Dad's proposal."

"It'll be good to do something less stressful for a while. I like the idea of focusing on one project and seeing it through to completion."

"You'll be working shorter hours."

"I know." His smile broadened. "I'll have lots of time to spend with my bride."

She straightened his bow tie. "I like the sound of that."

"What do you suggest we do about our wedding?"

She tilted her head sideways. "I can go to Queensland ahead of you. You can tie up all the loose ends here, make sure Sean is settled, and I can come back to Sydney for our wedding."

"You think you can organize everything from Queensland?"

She nodded. "Laura can help when she returns from her honeymoon."

"I guess she's now the wedding expert."

"I trust Laura to do a good job. She's reliable and she'll love being my matron of honor."

"Greg can help out, too. He'll have a few best man duties to fulfill."

She grinned. "I'm starting to like the idea of a smaller, more intimate wedding."

"You are?" He brushed his lips over hers, sneaking a kiss. His eyes twinkled. "I want us to enjoy our wedding. It should be a special day that we'll remember and cherish for the rest of our lives."

"It'll be easier to organize at short notice. In fact, I've already chosen a dress. I tried it on when I went wedding dress shopping with Laura."

"You wanted to marry me back then?"

She laughed. “It wasn’t my idea. The designer talked me into trying it on. She said it was made for me.”

“I can’t wait to see you wearing it.”

“I fell in love with the dress, and I’d hoped to wear it one day as your bride.”

He hugged her close to his side. “That day will be coming very soon. Now I have a surprise for you.”

She lifted her brow. “What is it?”

He shook his head. “Remember how I was telling you about the organization that helps families with loved ones struggling with addictions?”

“Yes, they do a lot of great work in the community.”

“Well, I’m financing a new program to help families in regional and remote areas who don’t have easy access to resources.”

Tears formed in her eyes. “Ryan, that’s fantastic. It means so much to me that you’re supporting those families.”

He nodded. “You mean the world to me, and what’s important to you is important to me. Besides, I can see that the program Sean’s doing is really helping him.”

“I’m proud of him, and the progress he’s making.”

“He could always move to Queensland with us. There’s an excellent surf beach near the resort.”

“Sean would like that.” She blinked away the tears, and her heart swelled. “I feel blessed that God has brought us together. I’m looking forward to our wedding day.”

Ryan grinned. “You’ll be the most beautiful bride ever.”

She couldn’t wait to marry her tycoon hero.

* * * * *